"Finely crafted . . . Mr. Ahmad writes with an insider's knowledge, a careful attention to detail, and an admirable restraint in his language. . . . This is how the tribes live, he says, neither romanticizing nor criticizing their way of life. *The Wandering Falcon* is not a long book. But it is dense with nuance and offers uncommon insight into a land too often explained away as 'the most dangerous place on earth.' A wonderful debut."   —*The Economist*

"Superb. The work of a gifted storyteller who has lived in the world of his fiction, and who offers his readers rare insight, wisdom, and—above all—pleasure."

—Mohsin Hamid, author of *Moth Smoke*
and *The Reluctant Fundamentalist*

"I've been talking about this book to anyone who will listen. . . . *The Wandering Falcon* is not only about tribes. It is about honor, love, loyalty, and grace. And it is about borders—geographical, political, and personal. The terrain where Pakistan, Iran, and Afghanistan meet may be cruel and unforgiving, but every page of this book is filled with beauty and humanity. By the final pages, I found myself transformed."   —Nami Mun, author of *Miles from Nowhere*

"Illuminates one of the most perilous regions of the world. . . . Engages your head as well as your heart. . . . The early chapters are reminiscent of masterpieces like Cormac McCarthy's *Blood Meridian*, which also features a boy alone in a gorgeous but harsh and often terrifying landscape. . . . [A]ll the way through, the characters, the tales, and the landscape are rendered with clarity, sympathy, and insight. The author makes us travel with him. . . . The book offers a rich picture of the 'mountainous, lawless tribal areas' we have previously known mainly for bullets and bombs."
—Steve Inskeep, NPR.org

"[I]n his stripped-down prose lies a beauty that is almost sublime."
—*The New Republic*

"Partakes of the power of myth and give[s] back to the reader the ambiguities of antique culture alive and well in the world of contemporary national borders. . . . Ahmad's voice is usually clear and sharp like the sound of plucked strings from a musical instrument."
—Alan Cheuse, NPR.org

"An accomplished and important debut novel. . . . [A] rare and sympathetic glimpse into a world that most Westerners know only through news reports related to military operations. . . . A fascinating journey; essential reading."
—*Library Journal* (starred review)

"In his first novel (at the age of eighty), [Ahmad] proves a masterful guide to the landscape and to the captivating art of storytelling at its finest. . . . A gripping book, as important for illuminating the current state of this region as it is timeless in its beautiful imagery and rhythmic prose."
—*Publishers Weekly* (starred review)

"A striking debut . . . Although the tribal areas of Pakistan have dominated the news and opinion pages for years, rarely has a writer shown greater empathy for its people, or brought such wisdom and knowledge to writing about a terrain largely inaccessible to journalists and writers. . . . Jamil's stories return the humanity to this devastated region. His characters defy the much-used categories of our times: moderates or extremists, Salafis or Sufis, pro- or anti-American. Their concerns are often ordinary, mostly difficult struggles for a life of dignity and love. . . . The power and beauty of these stories are unparalleled in most fiction to come out of south Asia."   —*The Guardian* (UK)

"[W]ritten with such a terrible beauty . . . The simplicity of the narration gives a fablelike effect to the storytelling. Its elegiac voice mourns the lot of the characters, yet refuses to judge the laws that trap them. They are neither romanticized nor vilified, but shown in all their terrible, resilient beauty."   —*The Independent* (UK)

The

WANDERING

FALCON

Jamil

Ahmad

RIVERHEAD BOOKS
New York

RIVERHEAD BOOKS
Published by the Penguin Group
Penguin Group (USA) Inc.
375 Hudson Street, New York, New York 10014, USA
Penguin Group (Canada), 90 Eglinton Avenue East, Suite 700, Toronto, Ontario M4P 2Y3, Canada
(a division of Pearson Penguin Canada Inc.) • Penguin Books Ltd., 80 Strand, London WC2R 0RL,
England • Penguin Group Ireland, 25 St. Stephen's Green, Dublin 2, Ireland (a division of Penguin
Books Ltd.) • Penguin Group (Australia), 250 Camberwell Road, Camberwell, Victoria 3124, Australia
(a division of Pearson Australia Group Pty. Ltd.) • Penguin Books India Pvt. Ltd., 11 Community
Centre, Panchsheel Park, New Delhi—110 017, India • Penguin Group (NZ), 67 Apollo Drive,
Rosedale, Auckland 0632, New Zealand (a division of Pearson New Zealand Ltd.) • Penguin Books
(South Africa) (Pty.) Ltd., 24 Sturdee Avenue, Rosebank, Johannesburg 2196, South Africa

Penguin Books Ltd., Registered Offices: 80 Strand, London WC2R 0RL, England

This is a work of fiction. Names, characters, places, and incidents either are the product of the author's
imagination or are used fictitiously, and any resemblance to actual persons, living or dead, business
establishments, events, or locales is entirely coincidental. The publisher does not have any control over
and does not assume any responsibility for author or third-party websites or their content.

The first chapter, "The Sins of the Mother," was first published,
in slightly different form, in *Granta* 112 (Autumn 2010).

Copyright © 2011 by Jamil Ahmad
Cover design by Evan Gaffney Design
Cover photographs: Mountains © Philip Poupin / Zuma Press;
Man © Edward A. Ornelas / *San Antonio Express-News* / Zuma Press
Book design by Nicole LaRoche

First edition: Penguin Books Ltd and Penguin Books India Pvt Ltd 2011
First American edition: Riverhead hardcover: October 2011
First Riverhead trade paperback edition: October 2012
Riverhead trade paperback ISBN: 978-1-59448-616-6

The Library of Congress has catalogued the Riverhead hardcover edition as follows:

Ahmad, Jamil.
The wandering falcon / Jamil Ahmad.—1st American ed.
p.   cm.
ISBN 978-1-59448-827-6
1. Nomads—Fiction.   2. Pakistan—Fiction.   3. Afghanistan—Fiction.   I. Title.
PR9540 9.A44W36 2011   2011030060
823'.92—dc23

PRINTED IN THE UNITED STATES OF AMERICA

10   9   8   7   6   5   4   3   2   1

To my wonderful family,

especially my wife,

Helga Ahmad

Contents

One

THE SINS *of* *the* MOTHER

In the tangle of crumbling, weather-beaten, and broken hills where the borders of Iran, Pakistan, and Afghanistan meet is a military outpost manned by about two score soldiers.

Lonely, as all such posts are, this one is particularly frightening. No habitation for miles around, and no vegetation except for a few wasted and barren date trees leaning crazily against one another, and no water other than a trickle among some salt-encrusted boulders, which also dries out occasionally, manifesting a degree of hostility.

Nature has not remained content merely at this. In this land, she has also created the dreaded *bad-e-sad-o-bist-roz,* the wind of a hundred and twenty days. This wind rages almost continuously during the four winter months, blowing clouds of alkali-laden dust and sand so thick that men can barely breathe or open their eyes when they happen to get caught in it.

It was but natural that some men would lose their minds after too long an exposure to such desolation and loneliness. In the course of time, therefore, a practice developed of not letting any soldier stay at this post for two years running, so that none had to face the ravages of the storm for more than one hundred and twenty days.

It was during one of these quiet spells that the man and woman came across this post hidden in the folds of the hills. The wind had been blowing with savage fury for three days, and had its force not suddenly abated, they would have missed the post altogether, and with it the only source of water for miles around. Indeed, they had steeled themselves to travel on during the approaching night, when the impenetrable curtain of dust and sand seemed to lift and reveal the fort, with its unhappy-looking date trees.

The soldiers, who had remained huddled behind closed shutters while the wind blew, had come out into the open as soon as the sky cleared. Sick and dispirited after three days and nights in darkened, airless, and fetid-smelling rooms, they were walking about, busy cleaning themselves and drawing in gulps of fresh air. They had to make the most of this brief respite before the wind started again.

Some of the men noticed the two figures and their camel as they topped the rise and moved slowly and hesitantly toward the fort. Both were staggering as they approached. The woman's clothes, originally black, as were those of the man, were gray with dust and sand, lines of caked mud standing out sharply where sweat had soaked into the folds. Even the small mirrors lovingly stitched as decorations into the woman's dress and the man's cap seemed faded and lackluster.

The woman was covered from head to foot in garments, but, on drawing closer, her head covering slipped and exposed her face to the watching soldiers. She made an ineffectual gesture to push it up again but appeared too weary to really care and spent all her remaining energy walking step after step toward the group of men.

When the veil slipped from the woman's face, most of the soldiers turned their heads away, but those who did not saw that she was hardly more than a child. If her companion's looks did not, the sight of her red-rimmed swollen eyes, her matted hair, and the unearthly expression on her face told the story clearly.

The man motioned for the woman to stop, and walked up, by himself, to the subedar commanding the fort. He kept a frenzied grip on the barrel of an old and rusty gun that he carried across his shoulders. He had no time to waste over any triviality.

"Water," his hoarse voice said from between cracked and bleeding lips. "Our water is finished, spare us some water." The subedar pointed wordlessly toward a half-empty bucket from which the soldiers had been drinking. The man lifted the bucket and drew back toward the woman, who was now huddled on the ground.

He cradled her head in the crook of his arm, wet the end of her shawl in the bucket, and squeezed some drops of water onto her face. Tenderly, and feeling no shame at so many eyes watching him, he wiped her face with the wet cloth as she lay in his arms.

A young soldier snickered but immediately fell silent as the baleful eyes of his commander and his companions turned on him.

After the man had cleansed her face, the Baluch cupped his right hand and splashed driblets of water onto her lips. As she sensed water, she started sucking his hand and fingers like a small animal. All of a sudden, she lunged toward the bucket, plunged her head into it, and drank with long gasping sounds until she choked. The man then patiently pushed her away, drank some of the water himself, and carried the bucket up to the camel, which finished whatever was left in a single gulp.

He brought the empty bucket back to the group of soldiers, set it down, and stood there, silent and unmoving.

At last the subedar spoke. "We have given you water. Do you wish for anything else?"

A struggle seemed to be going on within the man, and after a while, very reluctantly, he looked back at the subedar. "Yes, I wish for refuge for the two of us. We are Siahpads from Killa Kurd, on the run from her people. We have traveled for three days in the storm, and any further travel will surely—"

"Refuge," interrupted the subedar brusquely, "I cannot offer. I know your laws well, and neither I nor any man of mine shall come between a man and the laws of his tribe."

He repeated, "Refuge we cannot give you."

The man bit his lips with the pain that roiled within him. He had diminished himself by seeking refuge.

He had compromised his honor by offering to live as a *hamsaya*, in the shadow of another human being. He turned as if to move but realized that he had no choice but to humble himself further.

He once again faced the subedar. "I accept the reply," he said. "I shall not seek refuge of you. Can I have food and shelter for a few days?"

"That we shall give you." The subedar hastened to atone for his earlier severity. "Shelter is yours for the asking. For as long as you wish it, for as long as you want to stay."

There was a long line of rooms some distance away from the fort. These had been hastily constructed during the First World War, when the strength of this fort had, for a short period of time, increased almost a hundredfold. Sand had started collecting against the walls as soon as the construction was raised. Slowly and steadily, it had risen and, with no one to clear it, had reached roof level after a few years. With the passage of time, most of the walls and roofs caved in under its crumbling pressure. Now, nearly fifty years after the initial construction, mounds of sand occupied these rooms. However, there still remained a few that had not yet collapsed.

It was in one of these rooms that Gul Bibi and her lover were provided their shelter. For a few days, the couple hardly stirred outside their one small room. The only signs of life were the opening and closing of shutters as the wind died or strengthened, or when food was taken to the hut by the soldiers. Some time after the food had been left at the doorstep, the door would open furtively and the platter would be dragged in, to be pushed outside a while later.

As days passed, the couple appeared to gather more courage. They would occasionally leave the door open while the man stepped outside to look after his camel. Then one day the woman, too, came out to make a broom out of some thorn shrubs for sweeping the room. After a few days of inactivity, the man, of his own volition, started fetching water for the troops on his camel. He would load up the animal with water skins and visit the springs twice a day. Once he brought to the fort, as a gift, a few baskets, which the girl had woven out of date-palm leaves. "They are to keep your bread in," he explained to the soldiers. And this is the pattern life followed as time rolled by. Days turned to weeks and weeks to months. Winter gave way to summer. Some soldiers left as their period of duty ended. Others arrived to serve their turn at this outpost.

With each change—even the most minor—the couple appeared to withdraw into themselves for a while. They hardly ventured outside, and none of the shutters would open. Then, after some time, they would cautiously emerge and slowly adjust to the change. In this state, they reminded the soldiers of small, frightened desert lizards, which rush frantically into their burrows at the slightest sign of danger.

As each party of soldiers left, some would try to leave behind for the couple anything they could spare out of their meager possessions. A pair of partly worn-out shoes, a mended bedsheet, some aluminum utensils. These they would tie into a parcel and place at the doorstep of the hut before the army truck drove them away, back to the headquarters. Then the soldiers started taking up a collection on every payday and insisted on handing it over to the man for fetching their water. He had refused the money the first time, but as the soldiers appeared to get upset at this rebuff, he forced himself to accept the payment without expressing his gratitude in words. With no discernible expression on his face, he would take the proffered money, stuff it into a pocket of his tattered waistcoat, and walk away. Indeed, there were times when his look of infinite patience, aloofness, and lack of expression made some new arrivals among the soldiers feel uneasy. But as time passed, each new group would accept him, though they failed to breach the barrier he had drawn around himself.

The real change came with the birth of their child.

The soldiers had become accustomed to the same collection of drab buildings with their sullen and frustrated dwellers, each begrudging the days wasted at this bleak outpost and desperately longing for a return to more habitable places, to the sights and sounds of crowded bazaars, the smell of water and vegetation, the feel of clean, freshly laundered clothes, and the banter and sally in the shops. But with news of the birth, the air of resentfulness and bitterness, which seemed permanently to envelop this post, appeared to lighten.

To most of the soldiers, there was sheer wonder in the wizened looks of the infant, with his black locks of hair, as he was carried around by the mother. The baby's thin, plaintive cries brought back memories of their own families, whom they had not seen for years.

With the birth of their son, the couple, too, seemed to shed their fears. Indeed, they appeared to be relieved finally of their worries and tensions.

As soon as the season of sandstorms was over, the woman wove an awning out of desert scrub and rigged it over the door to provide protection from the strong sun during the coming summer months. She mixed some clay and water, and coated the room, the floor, and the door front with it.

She did more than that. She made a low wall about six inches high and enclosed an area the size of two beds in front of their room. She also made a gate into this small courtyard of hers—a gate with two small towers, each topped with a small round knob. After completing it, she stood proudly, waiting for her man to return in the evening to see her handiwork.

She had to wait for a long time, because his camel had wandered away while grazing. When he finally returned, he looked at her work for a long time before speaking. "My love, take away the towers, there is something about them I do not like."

She stood still for a while, and then, as the meaning sank into her, she rushed frantically toward them and crumbled them back into clay.

Subedar followed subedar as each year ended and a new one began. Indeed, the couple measured the passage of time by the change of subedars.

When the sixth one arrived, they realized that the boy was five years old.

A sprightly and active child he was, too. Fed on army rations, he looked older than his years. He spent his days inventing games of his own and playing them by himself or skipping from boulder to boulder, following the soldiers on their patrols. By the evening, he was generally tired and would creep into his mother's lap and sleep for a while before they started the meal.

One evening, when the man returned with water from the springs, the boy was still asleep in his mother's lap.

She turned as if to get up, but the man stopped her with a gesture. "Stay for a while, I like looking at you. There is an air of peace around you.

"I wonder what his life shall be when he grows up. What would you like him to be?" He looked at the woman.

She thought for a while. "Let him be a camel

herder, handsome and gentle as his father," the woman murmured.

"And fall in love with the sardar's daughter, his master's wife," the man countered.

"And carry her away," continued the woman.

"Into misery and sorrow and terror," flung back the man.

"Don't ever repeat this. You must never talk thus," she whispered.

The sleeping boy suddenly opened his dark eyes and said laughingly, "I have been listening to you, and I shall tell you what I will be. I shall be a chief, I shall have horses and camels. I shall feast your friends and defy your enemies, wherever they be."

Gently the woman pushed the boy away from her lap and started getting the evening meal ready.

One winter morning, while the couple was sitting in front of their hut, a camel rider suddenly appeared and rode his camel straight up to the fort. His arrival was so unexpected that it left them no time to hide. So they remained sitting impassively while the man finished his business and rode away without casting a glance in their direction. Nevertheless, as soon as the stranger rode over the crest, the couple gathered the child, who had been playing in the dust of the courtyard, and moved inside the hut, as though its chilly interior suddenly offered more warmth than the sun outside.

A little later, the subedar walked up to the hut and called the man outside. He wasted no time on preliminaries.

"That rider who has just left the fort was a Siahpad," the subedar told him. "He was asking questions about you. You know what that means?"

The man nodded dumbly.

"If you wish to leave," continued the subedar, "collect some food from the canteen. The men have packed a bag for you. If God wills, we shall meet again one day."

The couple departed on their camel at early dusk,

the man sitting in the middle with the boy perched in front and the woman behind him. Once again, the old familiar smell of fear was in his nostrils. The woman had asked no questions. She packed and dressed quickly, first putting warm clothes on both herself and the boy, and then making a light load of the few things that they needed to carry for their journey. The rest of her possessions, those collected over the past years, she neatly arranged in a pile in one corner of the room.

Her man had brought the camel around to the doorstep and made it kneel. He had cleaned his gun, and it was back on his shoulders. As she stepped out to mount the camel, she cast a quick backward look into the room, her glance briefly touching the firmly packed clay floor, the date-palm mats she had woven over the years, and the dying embers in the fireplace. Her expression remained as calm and serene as if she had been prepared for this journey for a long time.

The lone camel followed the lightly strung telegraph line for about twenty miles before the man decided to strike eastward into the broken country.

They tried to use their knowledge and wits to the fullest. They varied their pace, and changed direction frequently, and also the time of travel. They never spent more than the very minimum time possible at any water hole. When they rested, they chose the most secluded spot, and even there, they would pile up scrub and thorn brush to hide them and their camel.

They saw no signs of their pursuers, and after five days the woman became a little sanguine. "Perhaps the stranger was not a Siahpad. Perhaps we were not recognized," she remarked hopefully. "Perhaps he kept the news to himself. Perhaps they did not chase us. Perhaps they have lost us," she chanted.

"No," the man said. "They are after us. I feel it in the air."

The man was right. On the morning of the sixth day, as the couple was filling the water skin at a water hole, they saw their pursuers top the horizon.

It was still early morning, when the desert air is unsullied by the eddies of sand and the whirling of dust devils. The party was a considerable distance away, but there could be no mistaking who they were. The woman's husband and her father were riding their camels a short distance in front of the main body of men.

The man called Gul Bibi close to him. He placed his hand on her shoulder and looked into her eyes. "There is no escape for any of us. There was never any escape. You know what I have to do now?"

"Yes," she replied. "I know. We have talked about this day many times. But I am afraid, my love."

"Do not be frightened," spoke the man. "I shall follow you. I shall follow you soon." The woman walked away a few paces and stood there with her back toward the man. Suddenly, she spoke out again: "Do not kill the boy. They might spare him. I am ready."

The man shot her in the back while she was still speaking. He then reloaded his gun and looked reflectively at the boy, who stared back at him with unblinking eyes. With a shrug the man turned away, walked up to the kneeling camel, and shot it dead. He then stood together with the boy, waiting for the pursuers to reach him.

The party rode up to the water hole and dismounted. The old man was in the lead. He glanced at the sprawled body of his daughter and looked at her lover.

"Who is the boy?" he asked. His voice was cold and without emotion. The voice of a stranger. The inky black folds of the headgear hid half his face, but the eyes were the old familiar eyes that each man of the tribe knew. Eyes that could show anger, hatred, love, laughter, fondness, and humor more vividly than anyone else's. Now they showed nothing.

"Who is the boy?" the sardar asked again, his voice remaining flat, not even showing impatience.

"Your daughter's son," replied the man.

The boy stood shivering as the two men talked about him. He was nervously fingering a small silver amulet that hung around his neck on a gray-colored string.

The husband of the dead woman approached.

"Whose son is he?" he growled. "Yours or mine?" The lover did not reply, but his eyes again met those of the old man. "He is her son," he repeated, pointing to the huddled boy. "That silver amulet is hers. She must have placed it around his neck before her death. Do you not recognize the amulet? She always said you gave it to her to ward off evil spirits."

The old man said nothing but picked up a stone. His companions did likewise. The lover stood still as the first shower of stones hit him. He started bleeding from the wounds on his face and temples. There was another shower of stones and yet another, before he fell.

At first he lay half sitting and half sprawling. Then he lay with only his elbow supporting him. Finally, that small gesture of pride, too, failed him, and he lay stretched on the ground, his clothes darkened with blood and small rivulets of it running across his back, staining the ground. The hail of stones continued, with the circle of men moving closer and closer. The agony ended only with death, the bones broken and the head crushed beyond recognition.

After they had killed the lover, the offended husband turned to his companions.

"Now we start with the boy." The boy, who had been standing next to the dead camel, heard this and started whimpering.

"No," admonished the old man. "The boy's death is not necessary. We shall leave him as we found him."

Some of the other men murmured their agreement. "Yes, let him stay as he is," they agreed. "The sardar is right."

The party dragged the bodies a short distance away and entombed them separately in two towers made out of the sun-blackened stones that lay scattered in profusion all around the water hole. They used mud and water to plaster the towers so that their work might endure and provide testimony, to all who cared, about the way in which the Siahpad avenged insults. The old man took no part in the burial but walked about by himself. He did, however, interrupt his walking for a while, and stood at the spot where the bodies had lain.

As soon as the men had finished, they mounted their camels and rode away. After traveling but a short distance, the father of the dead woman suddenly reined in his camel.

"I should have brought the boy," the older man said, shading his eyes with his hand and staring in the direction of the water hole.

"Death would be best for the likes of him," burst out the son-in-law. "The whelp has bad blood in him."

"Half of his blood is my blood. The blood of the chiefs of this tribe. What mean you by 'bad blood'?"

"I still say what I said before," answered back the husband. "He has bad blood. Nothing good shall come out of him."

The sardar moved his camel up to the other man's as the rest watched him. He looked around. "Let me tell you all now," he shouted. "My daughter sinned. She sinned against the laws of God and those of our tribe. But hear this also. There was no sin in her when she was born, nor when she grew up, nor when she was married. She was driven to sin only because I did not marry her to a man."

He pointed a shaking finger at his son-in-law. "You know well enough what I say," he thundered, his emotions suddenly bursting out. "Marry another woman, marry as often as you like. Every one of them shall be driven to sin, for reasons you are aware of."

At this insult, shouted in his face before the men of his tribe, the face of the other man darkened with rage.

"You should not have said such things, old man, even if you be our chief," he shouted as he drew his sword quickly and slashed at Gul Bibi's father. Once, twice, thrice, he swiped, and the old man was already dead as he slid down in small jerks, like a broken doll, from the saddle to the ground.

With his death, the party scattered. The men did not wait to bury their chief's body in a proper grave but left it covered under a thin layer of sand, hoping the approaching sandstorm would bury it deeper. Whether fearful of the evil they had seen or afraid of being involved in another feud, or maybe weary of one another's company, they just rode away hurriedly.

At the water hole, the boy had stopped shivering after the party departed. He had overcome his fear and was sitting between the two towers, playing with some stones and quartz crystals. At first he had tried to prize some stones away from the towers, but they were too tightly wedged together, and his fingers made no impression on them.

As the sun rose higher, he sat quietly, watching the clouds of sandgrouse that appeared in the sky. Flight after flight alighted at the edge of the water hole, dipping their beaks in the water and flying away back into the sun. Their peculiar chuckling calls and the whirring of countless wings provided him some diversion from the horror he had just witnessed.

Then he was completely alone. The thousands of birds, which had kept him company for a while, had disappeared. With nothing to keep him occupied, he became aware of his thirst and hunger. He tried to resist it for a while, but as the pangs grew sharper, he finally walked over to the camel and opened the bag containing food. He ate a little, drank some water, and then lay down, squeezed against the dead camel, as the sandstorm approached.

Two

A POINT
of HONOR

The water hole lay in the area of the Mengals—
a Brahui tribe of Baluchistan.

A group of seven men and four camels had com-
menced their journey toward this oasis while the
stars still shone across the sky. From their last halt,
nesting among the gaunt ridges of sandstone, they
had debouched onto the plain as the day broke. Since
then, the party of Baluch had been riding their
camels through mile after mile of flat, desolate landscape, with only a few sand dunes to break the monotony. Patiently, they had skirted stretches of oily,

ocher-colored quicksand and had bravely pushed their animals through the bruising patches of camel-thorn bushes and burning salt flats.

The sandstorm had broken on them just as the camels were beginning to smell water. For hours, they had lain on the leeward side of a crescent-shaped dune. They muffled their faces and pressed themselves against their animals as the winds shrieked around them and the world turned dark.

The storm ended as abruptly as it had begun. The men unmuffled their faces, gratefully drawing in the fresh and clean air that follows in a storm's wake, and recommenced their wearisome trek.

This time the men walked. The water hole was only a short distance away, and the animals were tired. If a camel got lost, one man—if not two—would have to drop out. In such circumstances, a camel was not merely valuable, it was life itself.

Despite their raging thirst, the men did not hurry. The closer they came to their goal, the more patient they became. After every few yards, they would scan the horizon. The storm, which had just passed, would have blown away all traces of their track, yet even while they walked they tried to read the ground for any telltale signs of danger. It was at times like these, when one is tired, when one is close to rest, that death must be guarded against most.

Hunted as rebels for months, they had learned their lessons dearly. If a Baluch needed little water and food when on the run, they had learned to do with even less. Betrayed once by the flashing mirrors embroidered on their caps, they had shorn their caps of all finery and trinkets. The traditional black, red, and white of their dresses was by now stained with sweat and dirt to neutral hues. They had also learned to live a life without their women.

Yet the land—their land—had seen to it that beauty and color were not erased completely from their lives. It offered them a thousand shades of gray and brown, with which it tinted its hills, its sands, and its earth. There were subtle changes of color in the blackness of the nights and the brightness of the days, and the vigorous colors of the tiny desert flowers hidden in the dusty bushes, and of the gliding snakes and scurrying lizards as they buried themselves in the sand. To the men, beauty and color were rampant around them, even if the patches of decorative colored cloth had been unrelentingly shorn from their own clothes.

They were still some distance away when they observed the two stone towers. These towers had not been there when they had last visited this water hole a few months ago. The sight made them uneasy.

They approached cautiously, with two men acting as scouts well in advance of the rest of the party. On moving closer, they saw the dead camel with its long neck stretched limply on the ground. At the sight of this dust-colored mound of dead flesh, the party withdrew hurriedly and started riding a wide circle around the water hole, keeping it just in sight. They kept watching and listening carefully, and then decided to advance toward it after satisfying themselves that no life stirred for miles around and no alien sound disturbed the land.

Except for their leader, Roza Khan, all the men were armed. They were carrying muzzle-loading guns with sickle-shaped stocks. Two of the party had, in addition, curved swords without scabbards, tied with twisted woolen cords around their waists.

Roza Khan was an old man. His big frame and height were all that remained of the strength and prowess of his youth—that and his memories.

Overgrown cataracts in his eyes had made him virtually blind. Even in the strongest light, he saw only vague and half-formed shadows. If events had not obliged him to honor his commitments to his tribe, he would have liked to seek treatment at the mission eye hospital, which was set up every winter in a town three hundred miles to the south to provide relief to the desert dwellers. He would have liked to see things, colors, faces, again before he died. If matters settled themselves, he would get his eyes operated on next winter. In the meantime, he would have to continue as well as he could.

He was not a fighting man, and was certainly

proving a hindrance to the free movement of the rest of the party. Men might have to die because of him. They might have to pay with their lives for his errors of judgment.

Yet he well understood their need for him. They needed a symbol, and it mattered not to them what his age or condition was. He would stay with them even though he had no special wisdom to offer, either about the ways of the desert or the wiles of men. He knew that his people's sense of honor and grace were such that they would attribute all heroic deeds to him and all failures to themselves. Nor would they admit to any man that in reality he—their chief—was a creature to be pitied, that the man leading them was one who could not even guide his own camel without muted words of advice from his companions.

Three of the camels were slim-bodied riding animals with graceful necks and slender legs. The fourth was a transport camel. Ugly, thick-bodied, and large-footed, its present mood of ill temper was manifesting itself in the growling rumbles rising from its stomach.

The camels, like the men, had been equipped for the journey. Their finery and decoration had been carefully removed, any unnecessary metal which might sparkle or jingle had been left behind, their saddle loads reduced to the minimum.

Since there was no cover around the water hole, they were able to approach it without fear of an ambush.

They halted a short distance away and took down the water skins. Then one animal was brought to the water and allowed to swallow a few gulps before being led away. There was a rumor in the air that all the water holes were being poisoned so as to deny their use to the rebels. When the animal showed no ill effect, the party proceeded to decamp.

The routine had been established a long time ago.

Camels had to be unsaddled, watered, and hobbled. Their pitifully thin bags of provisions were opened, and small quantities taken out. One man was assigned to collect shrubs, another to build a fire from a tinderbox. Food had to be cooked and eaten hurriedly before the sun set.

While this was going on, one of the party walked over to the opposite edge of the water hole to take a closer look at the dead camel. There he discovered the small boy sleeping, pressed against the camel's belly.

The boy awoke suddenly as the man's hand touched his shoulders. When he opened his eyes and saw a stranger peering at him, he closed them quickly and screamed. The other men came running. The boy kept on screaming while they lifted him and carried him, struggling all the while, to the old chief sitting next to the fire.

As the boy was set down before him, the old man turned his blind, unstaring eyes in his direction. "Stop your crying, son," he said. "It is not good to hear a Baluch—even a child—cry."

Instantly, the boy fell silent, and Roza Khan, sounding both kindly and stern, added, "And there is another good reason for you not to cry. Wailing in a man is like honey in a pot. As honey attracts flies, so does wailing attract trouble. Now, tell me, how did you come to be here?"

The boy remained silent. At last one of the men spoke: "He chooses not to tell, but the story is plain enough. The two towers and the dead camel tell it. We have no need to ask him." The old man thought for a while. "We cannot leave him here," he said finally. "We will take him. If there is any food on his camel, add it to ours." As the men moved away, the chief muttered to himself, "There is surely some kind of an omen in this, though who can read if it be good or bad."

After finishing the meal, they sat around the smoldering embers and the stones, warm from the heat of the fire. The stars were out in their millions across the clear desert sky. Every now and then, a meteorite would streak across, burning brightly for an instant before it disappeared.

As they waited for Roza Khan to break the silence that had enveloped them, each man, oblivious to the others, started fashioning a small, strange structure on the ground in front of him. Starting with a flat stone to serve as a base, tiny rounded pebbles, sharp splinters of rock, wisps of straw, and twigs were patiently and with complete concentration being balanced and fitted onto one another. In fractions of inches, these diminutive structures were taking shape and rising out of the ground while the men sat. In the last few days they had come upon two travelers who had heard that the government was willing to hold discussions with them under a flag of truce, and to suspend hostilities while the talks lasted. In their whispered conversation they felt that Jangu, who was closest to the chief, would raise the subject on an evening of his choice.

They all knew that this was the evening they had to decide the one important thing that each one had been thinking about while keeping his mind veiled from the rest.

Roza Khan's dry, rasping cough suddenly shattered

their reveries. He cleared his throat and spat over his shoulder. "Which way do we go tomorrow?" he asked, looking around him. "Jangu," he said, staring toward his right. "You tell me what you think, Jangu."

The reply came from the man sitting next to his elbow. "Sardar," responded Jangu, "there is no simple answer. Let us talk about the things we know. Then I shall tell you about the things I alone know. After that, we shall make a decision."

"Yes, let us do that," responded Roza Khan.

Jangu Khan went on: "First, we all know the seed from which the trouble has grown. The officers of the district chose to remove and arrest the chief of our brother tribe. We allow the right to make and unmake chiefs only to ourselves. We do not accept the power of anyone else to decide who our chief shall be or shall not be. That is the cause, and we cannot help but fight for such a cause. Indeed, it is a cause of conscience."

"Conscience!" the old man's voice broke in. "Jangu, do not talk to me of conscience. What kind of a guide is it when it comforts the evil man in his labors no less willingly than another who struggles against wrong. Never have I seen a man truly troubled by his conscience. Conscience is like a poor relation living in a rich man's house. It has to remain cheerful at all times. It has to remain cheerful at all times for fear of being thrown out. Our cause is right, because we think it is right—but never depend on conscience, yours or another man's."

As he finished, two voices broke in eagerly. "Sardar," they pleaded, "please, let Jangu continue."

There was no impatience, only pleading, in their voices, but the old man felt immeasurably sad and lonely behind his curtain of darkness. *They do not understand,* he thought. *I hope to God there are people as full of doubts about right and wrong on the other side as I am.* "Continue, Jangu," he said wearily.

"So," Jangu went on, "six new moons have we seen since the trouble started. In this time, so many things have happened—mostly evil. Our crops have been burned, our grain stolen, and our animal flocks sold away or slaughtered. We have pointed our guns at them, and they at us. We have killed, and so have they. By now, even their airplanes hold no terror for us. All this we know, but now I shall tell you some things you do not know."

He had the full attention of the small audience now.

"Yes, Sardar. This you must know. Last week, I met a Baluch who is a charcoal burner near the big salt lake in the north. He told me that in our absence from our homes, our families have been made prisoners by the authorities. They—our women and children, even those remotely related to us—are living in jails. Bred and brought up in the deserts, they are now living and sleeping in evil-smelling dark rooms in the city."

A murmur swept the group of men.

"Yes," continued Jangu. "Our sardar is right in what he said. The men who did this remain glorious creatures in their own conscience."

He paused for a while and then went on again: "But I also heard another thing, which you do not know. This same Baluch told me that the officers have offered a safe conduct for us to hold parleys with them, so as to end our quarrel."

Jangu took out a soiled printed paper from within his shirt and carefully opened its folds. "On this paper is written the invitation and the safe conduct. Copies of this have been sent to many people."

None of the men could read or write, but each looked at the paper carefully and with seeming deliberation before passing it on to the next person.

The boy had been sleeping fretfully after his meal. As the talk drew toward its conclusion, he awoke and heard them decide to head to the headquarters of the authorities to discuss the terms of the safe conduct. They had agreed that their willingness to talk would not compromise their honor in any way.

On the evening of the third day, the Baluch led their camels into the town. The boy, who possessed no shoes, remained perched on one of the animals. They stopped at the first large building they saw. What seemed to them a palace was in fact the local post office.

Jangu went up the steps to a man standing in the doorway and produced the worn-out leaflet.

"Read this—we have come for the talks," he said.

The postmaster read the paper carefully. He looked at the men, excitement showing on his face. As he hurried to the telephone, he looked back and shouted, "Wait for the officers. They will be coming soon."

The seven men, the boy, and the animals were taken to a large house. For the next two days, they were given their meals, but no one came to see them. Each one of them was impatient about the delay but carefully hid his feelings from the others.

The pervading silence of their land had taught their people to be deliberate in their actions and slow in responding to emotions. They observed, though, that a party of soldiers had been placed around the house. Even this they avoided discussing with one another—much less mentioning it to Roza Khan. Finally, after the fourth day, they received some visitors, who brought a Jeep for them. The Baluch were asked to leave their guns and camels behind. They were driven for a while, until the vehicle entered a closed area surrounded by thick mud walls. The Jeep stopped at one of the buildings within the compound.

The room that they entered was full of people. Some were sitting on chairs, and others on benches. People were talking, and the conversation did not stop with their entrance. The men moved toward a part of the room that was bare, took off their shoes, and started making themselves comfortable on the floor.

Harshly, they were asked to remain standing. *It is a strange custom of these people,* they thought to themselves, *when one part stands and the others sit.* They were asked to swear an oath on the Koran that they would tell only the truth. This made them even more curious. *They swear by a book, while we swear by our chief—the sardar of our tribe.*

All the while, around them, the air remained thick with talk and laughter.

Then the charges were read out to them. They had

killed two army officers. "If proven guilty, you could die," they were told by a man sitting at a table on the other side of the room.

"Oh, no," Roza Khan protested. "We came for talks." He waved the paper in the direction of the voice that had addressed him. "Read this," he said.

"I know this paper," said the other man. "It is of no value. It carries no signature."

"Sardar, you speak for us," said Jangu, who was standing beside him. The others concurred in murmurs.

"Well, then I speak also for six of my companions."

"Seven," the boy interrupted.

"Seven," said Roza Khan. "I speak as their sardar, and I say that a word does not require a signature, nor a mark, nor yet an oath. The word was offered, and we took it."

"Do I have to write all that is being said?" asked the clerk petulantly.

"No," replied the magistrate. "Write only the things of importance. Thus far nothing has been said that needs to be written. You may merely say that the charges were read out and explained and the accused pleaded guilty."

"This is not what I said. Men were killed. Many men, not merely the two you speak of. Ours and yours. When my brother tribe was told that they would have a sardar no longer, could any man suffer such an insult? Has there ever been a Baluch who did not have a sardar?" Roza Khan fell silent.

"Have you more to say?"

"What shall I record?" asked the clerk again.

"I am wondering," said Roza Khan, "how to explain to you what a sardar is. If people in this room could be silent, thoughts shall come easier to me. We Baluch are used to the silence of the desert," he apologized handsomely, "and are not as clever as you."

The room fell silent. After a while, Roza Khan spoke again.

"I do not know what you would make of this tale, but it is said that each man needs a sardar, seeks and finds one for himself—a Baluch more than others. The story goes that Adam was the first Baluch on this earth. When he found that he was alone and there was none besides him, he was so desolate that he created one in his mind and called him Allah, thus making a sardar for himself."

The lines around Roza Khan's milky eyes etched themselves sharply as he came to the end of the story.

The boy looked toward Roza Khan. "It is a beautiful story, Sardar, but they are not writing it down."

"No, nothing has been written down so far," agreed the magistrate. "Fables have no use here. They are not evidence. Can a fable explain a death? Say something about the men who have died. How did they die?"

"All right." Roza Khan's voice suddenly seemed stronger than before. "I shall tell you something which you may like to write down. There has been killing, not a few men but many. I led my tribe into it. I killed men myself. My final crime has been that I have led my tribe into this last folly. I asked them to join these parleys. This terrible wrong and this misjudgment have all been mine—"

"No," the magistrate interrupted him. "That no

man can accept." He added the final ignominy: "For a blind man to claim that he killed, or that he was the leader, is an act of pride that has no substance." He turned toward the clerk. "Write down in the record that the accused admitted to the killings."

Before the evening lamps had been lit, the trial was over. The clerks had started to tie up the files and close the cupboards. They wanted to leave for their homes as soon as the sentence was passed.

The magistrate turned to the clerk. "Show in the record that only seven men were tried, and they pleaded guilty. Let the child go." He then passed the sentence of death and asked the staff to drop off the boy in the town on their way home.

There was complete and total silence about the Baluch, their cause, their lives, and their deaths. No newspaper editor risked punishment on their behalf. Typically, Pakistani journalists sought salve for their conscience by writing about the wrongs done to men in South Africa, in Indonesia, in Palestine, and in the Philippines—not to their own people. No politician risked imprisonment: they would continue to talk of the rights of the individual, the dignity of man, the exploitation of the poor, but they would not expose the wrong being done outside their front door. No bureaucrat risked dismissal. He would continue to flatter his conscience through the power he could display over inconsequential subjects.

These men died a final and total death. They will live in no songs; no memorials will be raised to them. It is possible that with time, even their loved ones will lock them up in some closed recess of their minds. The terrible struggle for life makes it impossible for too much time to be wasted over thoughts for the dead.

What died with them was a part of the Baluch people themselves. A little of their spontaneity in offering affection, and something of their graciousness and trust. That, too, was tried and sentenced, and died with these seven men.

———

When the subedar with the large mustache patrolled the town early in the morning, he recognized the small boy leaning impassively against the prison wall. The boy had been with the party of Baluch outlaws as they had walked proudly into the town. The subedar halted his patrol and walked up to the boy. "What are you going to do now?" he asked. "Your companions, they are all dead."

"I do not know," said the boy. Suddenly, he lifted his face. An eager look came into his eyes. "Can I go into the fort?" he asked, pointing toward the prison walls. The subedar looked closely at the boy to see if he was joking. Ghuncha Gul hated levity, but the boy was totally serious.

"No," he said quietly. "At least not yet. I am leaving this town, and you will come with me. The place I am going to is far away, but you and I might like it."

Ghuncha Gul ordered the patrol to start marching. He looked back and saw the boy following him.

Three

THE DEATH
of CAMELS

He called himself Sardar Karim Khan Kharot. By men of his tribe and all others, he was addressed as General. No man knew his age. If asked, he would grow reflective and say, "I know not. I can only say that I am in my third span. Two generations of men who roamed the earth with me have returned to their Maker, and I alone am left."

His hair gave credence to his tale. Even his eyebrows and eyelashes looked like patches of freshly fallen snow clinging bravely to a cliff face. But then his energy and vitality seemed to belie his claim as he led his nomadic tribe, year after year, on their seasonal migration from the Afghan highlands in autumn and their return from Pakistan after the winter was over, in early spring.

He was a familiar figure in all the lands through which his tribe ever journeyed. With a faded purple-and-gold cloak over his shoulders, he always walked in the company of his youngest son, Naim Khan, who was approaching fifty. A replica of his father, with the same square shoulders and stocky figure but a jet-black beard, Naim Khan called himself Colonel, and as with his father, no man dared ask him where he had obtained his rank. Since it was difficult to imagine either the father or the son submitting to discipline, it was generally assumed that they had received these honorifics as well as the elder's purple cloak from some long-dead king. If his tribe knew the secret, they chose to keep it to themselves.

The Kharot tribe numbered about a million men, whose entire lives were spent in wandering with the seasons. In autumn, they would gather their flocks of sheep and herds of camels, fold up their woven woolen tents, and start moving. They spent the winter in the plains, restlessly moving from place to place as each opportunity to work came to an end. Sometimes they merely let their animals make the decisions for them. When the grazing was exhausted in one area, the animals forced them to move on to another site.

With the coming of spring they would start back to the highlands, their flocks heavy with fat and wool; the caravans loaded with food and provisions purchased out of the proceeds from work and trading; men, women, and children displaying bits of finery they had picked up in the plains. This way of life had endured for centuries, but it would not last forever. It constituted defiance to certain concepts, which the world was beginning to associate with civilization itself. Concepts such as statehood, citizenship, undivided loyalty to one state, settled life as opposed to nomadic life, and the writ of the state as opposed to tribal discipline.

The pressures were inexorable. One set of values,

one way of life, had to die. In this clash, the state, as always, proved stronger than the individual. The new way of life triumphed over the old. The clash came about first in Soviet Russia. After a few years, the nomad died in both China and Iran.

By the autumn of 1958, with the British Empire dismantled and the once fluid international boundaries of high Asia becoming ever more rigid, both Pakistan and Afghanistan challenged the nomads. Restraints were imposed on the free movement of the Powindas, the "foot people."

The Kharots started moving from the highlands in the usual manner. Each *kirri,* comprising about a hundred tents, each one a day's march behind another, each with its own leader, converged toward Kakar Khorasan, the point at which they always crossed the border. Each tent meant a family. A family denoted not only the man, his wives, and his children but also his dogs and a few chickens, which the women generally insisted on carrying along with them. The dogs were a special kind of mastiff, savage and massive.

They had been bred over centuries, and were known as the Kuchi breed—the breed of the nomads.

A family also meant the accompanying herd of camels and flocks of sheep. These were usually kept together, and the animals of a *kirri* could number up to a few thousand sheep and a few hundred camels. Being kept together did not mean that the ownership was common, nor did it cause any confusion of identity. Not only the owner but also his five-year-old child could pick out their own animal from the herd without the slightest hesitation. While the General was the unchallenged head of the entire tribe, each *kirri* would also informally choose a leader to make the decisions for their group as they traveled.

It was the second day of the march, and Dawa Khan's *kirri* was settling down for the evening. The black woolen tents, open on all sides, had been pegged down and looked like rows of black bats resting on the ground. The smoke from the fires was swirling up into the folds of the tents, rolling out and drifting away with the light evening breeze.

The men were busy unhitching the panniers from the animals and bringing their loads to the tents, mostly carpets, dried fruit, and nuts, which they carried with them to sell in the cities. The women, too, were busy, cooking and milking the she-camels and sheep, or suckling their babies. Only the dogs were relaxed. They had done their day's work, ambling with the caravan, rushing sometimes to the front, sometimes to the rear, keeping the flock of sheep in order, traveling two miles for every one traveled by their masters. They were tired and needed their rest before they began their responsibility of guarding the camp during the hours of darkness.

Dawa Khan and his son carried in the last load and placed it in the tent of his younger wife. It was Gul Jana's turn to cook for the family that evening, but the other wife was helping her by baking the bread. The youngest child had crawled onto the dog, which had come with Gul Jana in her dowry. Gul Jana tasted the stew and added some more water.

Suddenly, the dog reared up, throwing the plump

child onto the grassy floor. His haunches tensed, and the ruff of his neck bristled. Dawa Khan and his son looked in the direction that the dog was staring.

The sun had not fully set, and while some areas were in shadow, the top of the mound in front of them was still covered with sunlight. As they watched, two figures gradually rose into view: an old man wearing a purple-and-gold cloak, with a black-bearded younger man behind him.

"The General and his son are here," Dawa Khan addressed his wives. "Prepare for their dinner tonight." As he started walking toward the mound, other men emerged from the hundred black tents and followed him. They met the visitors at the foot of the mound. For a few minutes, there was such a lively exchange of salutations and greetings that no one could actually hear what the others were saying.

After this tumultuous welcome had died down, the group of men started moving toward the tents, with Dawa Khan and the General in the lead. Most of the other men gradually fell back in ones and twos, returning to their own tents, till only Dawa Khan and four others remained.

At Dawa Khan's tent, some carpets had been spread on the ground, and two animal packs lay on the edges to serve as backrests. The men took off their shoes and sat down. The General, who, as always, kept his cloak on, looked at the men around him. They were old, familiar faces. He had known these middle-aged men since they were toddlers and had known their fathers before them. He smiled wryly at a hulking mustachioed figure sitting opposite him—this man, Torak Khan, had been so short in his childhood that he could not reach a camel's tail till he was thirteen.

"What is this story I hear about you?" the General inquired of him. "That you are suing another Kharot in the courts of the government?"

Torak grinned sheepishly. "The case is against a man who has left the fold," he replied defensively. "It is against a Kharot who is now settled in the city. He cannot really be considered a true Kharot any longer. The devil married my mother after my father's death and did not pay any bride price. As the eldest son, the money is due to me, and the man refuses to pay it. I have to get it out of him. My mother agrees with me."

"You are right, son," agreed the General. "No man respects his wife or her family unless he pays a price for her. But you should be able to get your due without seeking the help of other people's laws." He looked at Dawa Khan. "You will help him, of course."

"We will get his money," promised Dawa Khan.

The light faded away, and there was a sudden drop in temperature with the setting of the sun. A fire was started, and the sitting figures moved closer to it. As the dishes of stew and platters of bread were brought to them from the tents, the General turned to Dawa Khan.

"Your *kirri* is to lead the caravan this year."

"Yes, General."

"Be very careful and circumspect. There is to be no quarrel either among yourselves or with other tribes. No disputes with the authorities. I have heard a rumor that the authorities are going to demand travel documents from our people. You will continue moving while I go to the government officials to get a sense of things. Use your tact to the utmost, but also keep in touch with a few *kirri*s in the rear. Which are the *kirri*s nearest to you?"

"My father and brothers are leading the nearest, a day's march away," interjected Gul Jana, who was standing in the shadows, suckling her two-year-old. "Abdullah Khan and Niamat are following behind them."

"Very well. Ask Abdullah Khan to fall back. I want Niamat to be the third in the line."

The General then rose from the carpet and walked around the encampment, from one tent to the next. He had a word for every person, praising a man's rifle before his young sons at one tent, admiring a woman's son before the mother at another. He liked to see his people laughing and, as always, exchanged sallies with the women he knew in the various tents, including his granddaughter, who was resting after a difficult childbirth. But while the laughter was there, it sounded a little subdued to his ears. It did not sound like the open and unrestrained laughter that his ears were used to. Perhaps it was his imagination, but he even detected a small element of sadness and uncertainty in it. The words he had spoken on the carpet had by now, he was sure, spread to every tent. He only hoped he could come back to them and tell them that the rumor was false. But until he was able to do so, it was better for them to worry a little.

Early the next morning, while it was still dark and before the *kirri* was ready to move, the General and his son departed on foot, as usual. A few stars were still visible in the sky when they left, but the camp was humming with activity. The tents were already down and were being packed onto the animals. Some of the fires were being doused after the preparation of the morning meal, and the snorting of the camels intermingled with the barking of the dogs as they readied themselves for the journey. The caravan was to cross the border that day. The next day, they would know the attitude of the authorities.

The sun had not yet risen when the caravan started moving. By mid-morning they were on the edge of the plateau that marked the boundary between the two countries. A vast, flat plain—featureless except for small outcrops of rock breaking through the crust here and there. There was no sign of man in this area except for the ruins of a few *karezes*—underground channels tapping springwater for irrigation—which had been patiently constructed by a people long since vanished, and destroyed by another, also forgotten.

Today, all signs of cultivation and all marks of habitation had disappeared. A few springs, however, still remained, and the *kirri* stopped at one of these for their evening halt. The day had been entirely uneventful, and the people, who had been morose and edgy during the day, relaxed as the caravan paused and broke for the night. The men gathered together and talked for a while among themselves. They agreed that tomorrow would be an important day, and it was necessary that the young hotbloods should be kept in the rear while the elder and wiser men moved to the forefront.

Each man also agreed to keep a close eye on his sons and nephews, and to put them on their best behavior, so that their youth or exuberance did not create trouble for them all, in the event that they came across any government authority.

Within less than two hours' travel the next morning, the plain had ended and the track they had been following joined the bed of a dry ravine with a range of cliffs, interspersed by narrow valleys, on either side. Perched high on the cliff, guarding this gorge, was a small fort. It was built like an aerie anchored to black rock but jutting out at an angle into space.

As the caravan came into view, a long line of soldiers poured out of the fort and started scrambling down toward the Kharots. Dawa Khan stopped his caravan with a wave of his right arm and stood, looking toward the soldiers as they approached, led by their subedar, who was a familiar figure to them all, and famous in the area because of his mustache, which measured twelve inches from end to end.

As soon as he was within earshot, Dawa Khan shouted a greeting: "May you never be tired, Ghuncha Gul."

"May you never be weary, brother," responded the subedar. "Are you moving straightaway? My men are ready to escort you, unless you want to rest."

Dawa Khan's brow had cleared at the offer of the authority not only to allow them passage but also to protect them during their journey. Things sounded so normal that the rumors they had heard must indeed be wrong. Suddenly, Ghuncha Gul's voice broke in: "What is this I hear about the closing of the borders, Dawa Khan? One of my soldiers brought this rumor on his return from leave."

"I have also heard a rumor of this kind, and it had worried me somewhat. Do you think there is something to it?"

"I imagine not. It would be impossible to do that. It would be like attempting to stop migrating birds or the locusts."

They both laughed loudly for a while over this image. Dawa Khan then turned to Ghuncha Gul. "I did not forget my promise. I have brought a pup from my own dogs for your adopted son, as you had asked me. Where is the young lad? I would like to give it to him."

"The boy is in the fort," Ghuncha Gul replied. "He is going over his lessons with our mullah. I will hand him the pup on your behalf. He will value it."

Dawa Khan went back toward the rear of the long line of camels and returned shortly, half dragging a savage-looking young puppy, who struggled to free itself from the thick woolen cord tied around its neck. It growled furiously as it was handed over. Dawa Khan looked affectionately at the pup as he was led away. "I think he will make a good dog," he said. "He has got strength in his voice and a feeling of loyalty."

Ghuncha Gul and his soldiers spread out and took

up their escort duties on either side of the caravan. With a soldier walking alongside every fifty yards, the *kirris* were now under the formal protection of the government. The presence of the soldiers was intended to discourage raids by other tribes on the caravan; raids, with their resulting bloodshed and feuds, could cause problems for the government. Each fort was responsible for a part of the route. Ghuncha Gul would hand over safe custody of the caravan to the soldiers at the next fort, and the escort would turn back to wait for the next *kirri*.

Most of the soldiers in the twenty-man escort were familiar faces who were known to Dawa Khan. He had seen them over the years, in either one fort or another. They were a special breed of men. Tribesmen themselves, they spent their entire lives, from raw youth to middle age, living and serving on one mountain crest or another.

Except for short spells of leave to go back to their homes, they never saw their families. The only events in their lonely lives were protecting government roads and installations, laying down the law among the tribes, stopping bloodshed when it threatened to spill over from a family dispute into a tribal war, and their own postings and promotions. The only two recreations they had were listening to their radios in the evening and talking to strangers who passed through their area.

Gul Jana was sitting astride a she-camel with her two-year-old. The caravan was moving at a slow pace for the convenience of the soldiers, and she liked this lazy progress. The movement of the camel at this pace was not frantic and jerky. It swayed smoothly, as the ears of wild grass sway with a light breeze. Her child was asleep, and she, too, was feeling drowsy with the hypnotic rhythm of the camel's movement. She looked down from the camel's back to the right. This was the third time she had done so in the last half-hour.

The young soldier, who had been walking beside her camel ever since the caravan started moving, was still staring at her. He was short and slender, and looked very young with his light growth of beard, which would turn dark and heavy in a few years. The soldier colored slightly but could not seem to take his eyes off Gul Jana's face.

Gul Jana checked her camel slightly and straightened her back. "You, there!" She put a hand to the side of her mouth. "You, there, who has been staring at me for a long time. Do you not know that you are smaller than my husband's organ?"

The women on the camels behind her and those in front erupted into boisterous laughter, as did the men, including the soldiers within earshot. Gusts of laughter swept the caravan as the story passed from camelback to camelback and man to man, and soon everyone was laughing, except the lonely soldier, who wanted only to sink into the ground and die.

Ghuncha Gul knew what the young soldier was feeling. His own wife in the village, whom he visited for only one month every year, was somber and staid, and smiled rarely. The women of the plains kept to themselves, and were severe and serious in their demeanor. He decided not to commiserate with the soldier. That gesture might hurt him all the more, and, in any case, it was better for the boy to suffer the jolt of the ribaldry and boisterous humor of the Powindah women before he made any serious mistakes.

By the afternoon, the caravan with its escort had reached the next fort, which was also the headquarters of the delousing party working on the caravans using this trail. These groups of paramedics were responsible for ensuring that the nomadic men, women, and children were rid of the vermin that were believed to be carriers of typhus fever.

This was the point where Ghuncha Gul and the platoon took their leave. Another two marches brought the caravan to the outskirts of the largest fort in the area, Fort Sandeman, around which a settlement of sorts had grown. With the progress of each day's march, the caravan seemed to shed its fears slightly, and, while maintaining their contacts with the *kirris* following them, they gradually began to discount the rumors that had hounded them at the start of their journey. Except Dawa Khan. He could not relax totally—at least not until he had heard from the General. He felt it would be worthwhile to halt his people for a few days' rest at Fort Sandeman to wait for some news, to allow the women, children, and animals to recoup their vigor and to fulfill his commitment to the General to secure Torak Khan's bride price from his stepfather.

When he announced his decision to the *kirri*, there was considerable jubilation; the happiest were the women, who insisted on moving toward the nearest clump of trees. They wanted to have sturdy branches around them, on which they could hang their children's cradles. In their minds, home and permanency meant only a stay long enough to wash clothes or to affix the cradles to the trees.

On his way to the town the next morning, Dawa Khan and his companions took a detour up a narrow valley through a Kakar settlement, where he had another errand. He had sworn to avenge the murder of a cousin who had been killed by a Kakar tribesman years ago. The murderer had died a natural death soon afterward, leaving behind a widow and two young sons. As Dawa Khan turned the corner toward the house of the long-dead Kakar, he saw two tall, grown-up teenage boys sitting in front of the house. They were wearing only long shirts and had no trousers on.

"May you never be tired, Uncle!" they shouted in unison, as they recognized Dawa Khan. They were laughing as the greeting was given.

"May you never be weary," responded Dawa. There was acute disappointment in his voice. He came up here every year, hoping that the boys would take to wearing shalwars, signifying their having grown up, so that he could avenge his cousin. The Pushtunwali, the traditional code of the Pashtuns, was clear that revenge could not be visited on women and children. The wearing of a shalwar signified a transition into manhood, yet year after year the boys cheated him by refusing to wear trousers. For all he knew, these perfidious Kakars might well refuse to wear shalwars in his lifetime.

"How they tempt me to break our traditions," he said, and grunted, within hearing of the boys. The boys only laughed and were still laughing as the party turned the corner on their way back.

T he General and his son had been on the road for days but remained as vague about the question in their minds as they had been when they had set out on their journey. In one village they would be welcomed as old friends; in another, someone would ask them what they were doing there, and their fears would return, for they had crossed the international boundary into Pakistan. However, since this was the first year of the new policy on the frontier, and the border posts were not yet familiar with its precise terms, the lines of demarcation between the tribal areas and the settled districts were confusing to all. So it was in the government offices, too. The reactions of the officials alternated between the familiar welcome and point-blank questions as to how they had managed to cross the border. Their bewilderment increased with each passing day, as did their worry about what was happening to the caravans behind them.

One day, after being made to wait for a few hours on a bench, they were allowed to meet with an officer who was dealing with the tribes and the administration of the border. If anybody knew, it would be him. Both father and son wanted to hear the truth, even if it was unpleasant, rather than endure further uncertainty.

They had known the officer for years. He looked up as the General and his son walked in, and invited them to sit down. They exchanged pleasantries for a bit, but their forced attempts at treating this as an ordinary visit petered out after a short time. The General kept marshaling his thoughts. He finally realized that there was no way but to put the question directly and frankly.

"Tell me, sahib," he said, looking up, his face rigid with concentration, "do you know anything about this rumor of government orders against the Powindas?"

The officer held his gaze. "It is correct, Karim Khan, the government has indeed decided that there should be no movement between the countries without travel documents. And this affects you directly. A part of me is unhappy and sad at this decision, Karim Khan, but time passes, and events and men have to change with it. You and I cannot prevent this change even if we wish to."

The General and his son looked steadily at the official. At last the son spoke: "How is it possible for us to be treated as belonging to Afghanistan? We stay for a few months there and for a few months in Pakistan. The rest of the time we spend moving. We are Powindas and belong to all countries, or to none," he added reflectively.

"This argument has been used, and it did not count," the officer remarked.

"What will happen to our herds?" the General broke in. "Our animals have to move if they are to live.

To stop would mean death for them. Our way of life harms nobody. Why do you wish for us to change?"

"All these arguments and more have been put forward by your friends, General," the officer told him. "They are not acceptable to the government. The decision has been taken and cannot be changed. You will now have to accept it and try to live with it."

Father and son rose from their chairs. The General adjusted his cloak over his shoulders. His eyes seemed to be looking into the distance as he turned. "How is it possible? How could it happen?" He was addressing no one in particular. The son watched the father from two paces away, as he had done for most of his life. The General once again adjusted his cloak, and his son felt a stabbing pain as he realized that within the last few minutes this garment, which had signified grandeur, pride, and strength, had become an ordinary covering for an old man seeking to hide his mind and body.

The two men stepped onto the street feeling impotent and powerless, and began to walk along. Naim

Khan broke the silence, which had dropped like a curtain around his father.

"Shall we send word to Dawa Khan?" he asked.

"What can we tell him?"

"The truth," replied the son. "What else?"

"How will it help him? The animals are going to die. Hundreds of them."

"Yes, but Dawa Khan must know the truth."

They walked along silently for a while, thinking about the effect the new policy would have on them and their people. There was no way for them to obtain travel documents for thousands of their tribesmen; they had no birth certificates, no identity papers or health documents. They could not document their animals. The new system would certainly mean the death of a centuries-old way of life.

Then Naim Khan spoke again: "Cheer up, Father," he said. It was the first time in his life that he had addressed the General as such. "We shall go to the capital of this country and see their king. He will listen to you." He paused. "Yes, he surely will, Father."

Naim Khan's voice was pleading. He wanted to conjure the General from this beaten and tired old man.

Meanwhile, in Fort Sandeman, Dawa Khan kept waiting for a message from the General. He had used these days to good advantage. Torak's troubles had been sorted out. His stepfather had been made to agree to a handsome bride price. Collection of debts due from some local people had been carried out without trouble, and there were a number of successful sales of dried fruit and nuts in the local market.

During this time, three more *kirri*s had reached Fort Sandeman, and all around the settlement there was a girdle of camel herds and flocks of sheep. Dawa Khan was growing restive. With the increase in the number of animals, the grazing was depleting very fast, and already there had been occasional flashes of temper when the herds of one *kirri* encroached on the rights of another.

The message sent by the General reached Fort Sandeman late in the evening. A dusty old man, wheezing with asthma, brought it, descending from a ramshackle bus while people rushed off to fetch Dawa Khan. When Dawa Khan arrived, the messenger passed on the communication hurriedly, as the bus was waiting for him and the driver was blowing the horn impatiently.

After the bus left, the men started walking back to the encampment. Torak broke the silence: "Did you notice one thing, Dawa Khan? The General has sent no clear directions and no advice."

"We all did," replied Dawa Khan quietly. "He has left it to us to decide what to do. It is for us to make up our minds."

"It is not like him to act thus," Torak insisted. "The General has always made the decision."

"I know, I know," Dawa Khan soothed him. "But this time he wants us to decide. Let us not pass our own burden on to someone else. Let us decide for ourselves. We shall meet after the evening meal."

When they assembled after the evening had turned into night, Dawa Khan told the men about the news he had received from the General's messenger. "The General has sent no word beyond what I have told you. He has sent no instructions and no advice, and he clearly wishes we make a decision ourselves. The decision is not an easy one, but decide we must, as we have overstayed our welcome in this town and the grass is giving out. We have to move, whether it be forward or backward. If we move back toward Afghanistan, we will be wandering aimlessly until the winter is over and the snow melts in our highlands. These winter months will be bitter for us and our herds. We will not earn anything, either through trade or labor, and our animals will have to go hungry, as they shall be denied the pastures in the plains.

"Then there will be those among us who will argue that we have traveled far and it should not be without purpose. They will say to themselves that the plains are only a short distance away, and once we, our herds of camels, and our flocks of sheep move into the plains, we can scatter and no one can round us all up and take us back. If we manage to do this, they will also think we will be able to pass one year, and who knows what might happen the next year. To them I will only say that we must think carefully. Our journey from now on will not be carefree and easy, like a farmer wandering in his fields or like an eagle wheeling in the sky. From now on, all eyes will be on us, and we shall be like a thief running in a city street with a mob after us. He cannot hide himself, because on either side of him are brick walls or closed doors. In such a case, friends, if the poor thief finds a brick wall standing in front of him, he dies. The mob kills him. This is the situation. Between us and the plains are two forts. They shall be waiting for us. They must have clear orders by now, and it shall be their business to stop us. What say you?"

There were indeed two options, but to the men sitting huddled together with the firelight flickering across their faces, the first option did not exist. Hope does not die like an animal—quick and sudden. It is more like a plant, which slowly withers away. There was no voice raised in favor of the first choice. If there was anyone who had doubts, he kept them to himself. So it was decided to move forward.

The next morning the caravan ostensibly turned back, on the road toward Afghanistan.

Then, a few miles outside the town, they wheeled back toward the route leading to the plains in Pakistan. The maneuver seemed to work, because they were not pursued. After two days of traveling, while still short of the first military fort, they found a line of soldiers drawn up in front of them, blocking their path.

"You cannot cross," the soldiers told them. "We have our orders."

"What happens if we try?" asked the Powindas.

"We have been told to shoot, if necessary. The orders are very clear," said the subedar in charge dolefully. "Don't make it difficult for us."

"It is difficult for us, too," remarked Dawa Khan. "Our animals have been without water for more than two days, and they will not last if we turn them back now. Let us water them at the springs near the next army fort, and then we shall turn them back."

"I cannot let you do that," said the subedar. "I have to do as I am told."

"But our animals will die without water. You don't want to kill them."

"I tell you I have no choice. I cannot let you pass."

"All right," said Dawa Khan. "We have heard you, and you have heard us. We shall camp here for the night."

That night the caravan rushed past the fort. The officer in charge was dismissed through a wireless message the very next day. There was now only one fort left between the Powindas and the plains, if only they could cross it. Dawa Khan's leading *kirri* reached the fort before first light, but the soldiers were ready for them. The moment they heard the movement of the herds, they started firing star shells.

A voice from an amplifier announced, "This is a warning. Turn back. Move forward at your own risk."

"All right, all right," Dawa Khan shouted back

through cupped hands. "Let us water our animals and we will turn back."

"Oh, no, you shall not!" returned the amplifier. "We will not be taken in by your tricks."

"We shall turn back. I promise you," shouted Dawa Khan. "Our camels should not die without water."

"You cannot move forward. If you do, we fire. Understand that clearly," roared back the amplifier.

The women had been listening to this exchange between their men and the soldiers. Gul Jana called out to her husband, "Dawa Khan, I am going forward. The camels must not die. I am going with a Koran on my head. Nothing can happen to me." She separated about two scores of camels and, with Dawa Khan walking beside her, started herding the animals forward. They had hardly gone fifty yards when two machine guns opened up from either side and mowed down the camels. The firing was indiscriminate. Men, women, and children died. Gul Jana's belief that the Koran would prevent tragedy died, too. Dawa Khan fell dead in the raking fire.

The Powindas made two more attempts, and more camels died each time. After the third try, the Powindas started their trudge back. By the time they reached Fort Sandeman, hundreds of dead camels and sheep had fallen by the wayside. By the time they reached the border, most of the animals of the three *kirri*s were dead.

They say that the soldiers from the forts had to move out two days after the Powindas departed. The stench from the dead animals was so terrible that it was driving the soldiers mad. They also say that while the camel bones and skulls have been bleached white with time, the shale gorge still reeks of death.

As the General and his son started their journey northward, the air was thick with rumors. They followed them everywhere. Whether on roads, or in villages and hamlets, or in crowded city bazaars, there was no escape.

"The Nasirs have been mauled at Khojak Pass,

disarmed, and pushed back," whispered a camel trader at Pishin.

"The Dottanis almost reached the plains but were rounded up before they could scatter," claimed a traveling well digger near Gulistan. "Their leaders have been jailed. If this is not true, my wife be considered divorced from me." He picked up three pebbles and ritually dropped them one by one on the ground, signifying the divorce, and walked away. Rumors buzzed, but the father and son walked on. They spoke to each other only about normal, ordinary things.

"Will you eat?"

"Shall we rest?"

"Hamidzai Lora is in flood."

"Hailstorms will destroy the poppy crop this year."

"Prices of wool are higher this season."

It was when they had finished eating their evening meal and Naim Khan was getting up to wash the dishes that his father halted him peremptorily. Naim Khan sat down again and waited for his father to speak. "Tell me," asked the General, "when we breasted our way through the news and rumors, why did you not say to me such rumor is wrong and such rumor may not be right?"

"Because you are the General. The judgments are yours. You need no protection. You provide protection to all."

Karim Khan looked steadily at his son and then smiled affectionately. "Yes, you did not fail me, nor will our people. There are a hundred and one ways open to a man if he has the will to move."

The General mused for a while before he spoke again. "Remember, once when you were a lad of only five summers, that I took you to meet Painda Khan, the old man of the Kharots who had crossed his hundred summers? And you sat in the old man's lap and asked him, how can a person become so old?"

Naim Khan nodded silently.

The General's voice rolled on: "Remember what the old man said? His face brimmed with laughter as he turned to you and answered in a serious manner. 'The secret is raw onions. I eat raw onions and I survive.'

And then, over your head, his eyes met mine and we understood each other. What he told you that day was the secret of life itself. One lives and survives only if one has the ability to swallow and digest bitter and unpalatable things. We, you and I, and our people shall live because there are only a few among us who do not love raw onions."

It was not many days after this incident that Ghuncha Gul called the boy and the mullah to his room in the fort. "I am leaving," he told them. "I have been relieved of my duties here, and I am going back to my village. I have to start living my life again with my family. There will not be room in my life for an adopted son."

The boy gazed back steadily at the old subedar, who had been his protector since his companions were executed. The mullah spoke up: "I have looked after this boy for some time now, and I have found in him an intelligence I have rarely seen, and I like him. He can come with me if he so pleases. Where God in his bounty provides food for one person, He shall surely provide for two."

"Are you leaving, too, Mullah Barrerai?" inquired Ghuncha Gul.

"Yes, I am off on my wanderings again. I have stayed long enough at this place. Do not worry about this boy. His fortune will provide for him what is writ. You can go back to your village unburdened with an adopted son."

The mullah turned to the boy and placed a hand on his shoulder. "Come with me. Pack your things, we leave in a few hours."

The boy started to follow the mullah but then turned around and looked back at Ghuncha Gul. As their eyes met, he gave a brave smile. "Good-bye, Subedar," he said. "May you have all the good fortune in your village."

"God protect you," responded Ghuncha Gul, and he noticed that the boy did not address him as "Father," as he had always done. In less than an hour, the mullah left the fort with the boy walking beside him and the little puppy, who had been with his new owner less than a month, trotting behind.

The subedar stood in the shadows behind one of the embrasures and watched them until they disappeared from view. He was dismayed to see that the boy and the mullah seemed to be in good spirits. They were chattering continuously, and not once did the boy look back, not even for a last glance at the fort where he had spent two years of his life. *Such is gratitude,* Ghuncha Gul thought.

B oy," the mullah asked, as they were leaving the fort, "how old would you be?"

"By my reckoning, I should be seven years old."

"Ah," remarked the mullah, "this is truly wonderful. Today is the seventh day of the seventh month in our calendar, and you are seven years old. Do you not know that seven is a holy number? There are seven days in a week. There are seven skies. Indeed, there are seven veils between man and God, as also between man and himself."

"I know not this," came the confused reply.

"You are ignorant in some ways. Yes, it is so. Know this. Must I also tell you that today one of those veils has been lifted? As each is drawn away, you shall move closer to knowing yourself."

"I know not these things," cried the boy in a worried voice.

"I shall teach you such things and many more," promised the mullah. Thus absorbed in the conversation, the two rounded a bend in the ravine and went out of view of the old subedar.

Four

THE MULLAH

The drums started beating in a Bhittani village late one evening. Their booming notes could be heard throughout the night, rolling over the hills, with intermittent periods of rest to enable the drumbeaters to rebuild their rhythm and energy. As the somber thudding beat of the drums permeated the airless mud houses and hill caves where the families of the tribe lived, the men shook themselves awake, grabbed their weapons, and hurried out into the night, toward the source of the sound. In some cases it was the women who woke first, and it was they who shook the sleeping men, angrily admonishing them for their tardiness, and sped them on their way.

The drums signaled danger to the tribe. One man from every household in the vicinity had to respond to the call, armed and ready to fight. By the morning light, about three scores of men—the entire armed strength of the nearest three valleys—had gathered at the village. The Bhittani *chigha,* the fighting men, had collected.

The men were acquainted with the reason for the summons as soon as they arrived. A boy who had been sent out to graze his flock had not returned. His relatives had searched for him, but though they had found the animals wandering around, there was no sign of the boy.

The *chigha* started its search shortly after dawn. They scoured the hills, the dry, rocky ravines, and the gulches. Of the leading group, one was an adept tracker, but the hard, gritty soil gave him no assistance. The spoor of the boy had faded out soon after they reached the spot where his grazing animals had been found.

It was mid-afternoon, when some of the party were already thinking of resting for a while, that the discovery was made. In one of the blind ravines, half surrounded by thorn scrub, a bareheaded, bearded man was sitting on a flat slab of rock. The disemboweled body of the missing boy was stretched in front of him, while another, still alive, was bound to a tree with the man's turban a short distance away.

The man made no attempt to run as the party approached him. He remained sitting calmly on the rock. There was a glaze of madness in his eyes, and he continued running his fingers through his beard and smiled, although dozens of voices were shouting questions at him. After a while it was clear that the man— whoever he was—had lost his sanity and no longer saw or heard anything.

The relations of the dead boy shot the man in their rage, though once they had done so, they felt terribly afraid. It was believed that madness signified closeness to God, and anyone harming a mad person was inviting His wrath. They then freed the other boy, who had remained bound to the tree while all this was going on. He was young, hardly twelve or thirteen years old, and he wore a small silver amulet on a string around his neck. They assumed that he was another prospective victim of the madman. The boy spoke and understood their language, but his accent was strange and puzzling to them, and they could not place his tribe. Nor could the boy tell them where he had come from so that he could be returned to his parents.

They took back the body of the dead victim, as well as the other boy. The body of the bearded madman was left lying at the spot, hurriedly covered with stones and boulders. The parents of the dead Bhittani boy accepted the newcomer into their family. They gave him the name that their son had borne, Tor Baz—the black falcon.

While he did not tell them anything about himself, he did tell them the dead man's name.

"He was called Mullah Barrerai," the boy whispered one day to his adopted mother.

"Mullah Barrerai." Her voice sounded puzzled.

Then a half-forgotten memory struggled to the surface, and she suddenly started shaking with suppressed excitement. She scuttled to the opening of the cave and called out loudly to her husband, "Tor Baz says that the man you killed was Mullah Barrerai. Barrerai the Accursed, Barrerai the Devil!"

The man rushed into the hut and caught the boy's shoulder. "Are you sure?" he asked frantically. "Tell us more. Did he say anything to you about his gold? Tell us all you know about him. Did he talk about the past to you, the evil old man?"

Bewilderment showed on the boy's face. "He spoke of no gold. He spoke of the past, and he was not an evil man. Do not revile him, for he looked after me when I was left with no one. Then the madness struck him. Gold and money meant nothing to him."

"Ha," scorned the woman. "Tor Baz, you do not know the mullah. He was the devil incarnate. His greed is a byword among the tribes. He stole our gold. Truly, he cast a spell on you."

"No," insisted the boy firmly. "I knew all there was

to know. The mullah was not an evil man. May God forgive you for the injustice you do to him."

Tor Baz lived with the Bhittanis for about two years. One day, his foster father again pressed him hard to reveal his tribe. He remained stubbornly silent. The next day, he disappeared.

Strangely enough, while no one expressed any interest in the living boy, the dead mullah was not forgotten. Long after his death, strangers would visit the Bhittanis to question them about the circumstances of his death. There was also an old Scouts officer who a few months later prepared a proper grave for him. He would visit the grave regularly every year after that, standing for a while and going away without speaking to anyone.

At first the Bhittanis scarcely paid this visit any more attention than they did to the others. But after a few years, when his visits did not cease, their curiosity got the better of them. One year, the Bhittani headman could not restrain himself and accosted the visitor as he was leaving the grave after saying his prayers.

"We have all wondered about you, stranger," he addressed the visitor. "Why do you visit this grave so regularly? How well did you know this man? How can one who lived so evil a life find so devoted an admirer in you after his death?"

"Malik of the Bhittanis, I indeed knew him. I knew him well, and when you call him evil it pains me. I shall tell you the story, because a lifetime has passed since it happened, and it matters not today who knows it and who does not. Listen now. It was in the time when the British were still ruling in India. I was a young army officer then, a lieutenant in the Scouts, when I first met Mullah Barrerai. It so happened that one year some friends of mine and I decided to spend the Christmas week stalking mountain sheep. It was a delightfully successful week, because with the snow driving the animals lower and the mating season making them less wary, we were able to spot some really fine heads and bag some of them. One evening we returned to our camp a little earlier than usual. As we were camping near a village, some whim made us decide to say our evening prayers in the local mosque.

"The mosque was fairly big by village standards. With a tight squeeze, it could have packed the total male population of the village—say, about forty men. The prayers started almost as soon as we arrived, and we were prepared to get up and leave the moment they were over. However, to our puzzlement, we found that the rest of the congregation remained sitting and the village mullah started on a sermon. This was certainly strange, as we had never heard of a sermon after evening prayers. Anyway, I was glad that we stayed, because it was a very unusual sermon, indeed.

"First he told us a story about a man in these hills who was very poor. He told us that this man used to eke a living out of collecting firewood, which he would carry on a donkey—his most valuable possession— and hawk the firewood from place to place. When night came, he would spread his blanket under one tree or another and go to sleep for a few hours.

"'Friends,' the mullah told us, 'this man lived a lonely life. His parents were dead, and his brothers, sisters, and cousins had moved away to distant places. His poverty did not permit him to take a wife. One would suppose that such a man would have been unhappy. But this was far from true. He accepted his lot with happiness and joy. He was always full of gratitude and praise for his Maker, although another person in his place would have grumbled. He said his prayers regularly and always had a prayer for other people—never for himself. Looking at him, one would think that here, perhaps, was a truly contented man. And indeed this would have been so, except for a strong desire which this man possessed. He had only one secret wish. While he knew that it was impossible that this dream would ever be fulfilled, occasionally he would indulge himself in a vision of the pilgrimage to Mecca. He knew that for a poor man like himself to have such thoughts was a sign of weakness and a wrong thing to do, but he hoped that God would forgive him, as his thoughts were not wicked. Well, brothers! One day, when this man was sitting under a tree, lost in his thoughts, a voice suddenly appeared to speak to him. "Get up, go to your donkey, and it shall take you for a pilgrimage," it commanded. The man was bewildered, but did as he was told. As he approached the donkey, its stomach seemed to open up. The bewildered man sat down in it, and the walls of the stomach closed around him. The donkey then started trotting, and, believe me, it took him straight to Mecca, and the poor man performed hajj. This man died long ago. He must surely be resting in paradise. After his difficult stay on earth, I can imagine him sitting with the houris, who are wondrous, fair, and who possess breasts the likes of which are beyond your imaginations. Breasts so large that it would take a crow a full day and night to fly from one nipple to another. I can imagine him roaming in a cool forest where trees bear grapes the size of water pitchers and one grape can provide you your fill of food and water, and bath, too, if you wish it.'

"As the story ended, the enraptured audience let out an audible sigh of exhilaration and dispersed slowly, while we walked back to our camp, discussing the village mullah. By the time we reached our camp, we had decided to invite the mullah over to dine with us. Our messenger returned almost immediately and told us that the mullah asked what was cooked for dinner, and would come only if it included meat.

"Mullah Barrerai, as he introduced himself, liked his food and proved to be capital company. It was also quite a surprise for us to discover that he was totally free from prejudice. We were strangers in the area, but as the conversation progressed, we became a little bolder and started a discussion with him on the sermon of the evening. 'Tell us, do you believe in the story about the donkey?' I asked him.

" 'No,' came his quick reply.

" 'Do you believe in houris with chests as broad as you described, or grapes the size of water casks?'

" 'No.'

" 'Then why did you tell these lies?' I asked him.

"At my question, Mullah Barrerai started laughing. 'You don't understand,' he said. 'These are not lies. These stories are like ointment, meant for healing, or like a piece of ice in the summer, with which water in a glass is cooled. Would you call that piece of ice a lie?' He continued to tell us, 'What do these people have? Hardly enough food or water in normal times, and after a few months, summer will be upon them, when most of their springs will dry up. For the next few months, they will need hope as a thirsty man in the cities needs ice in his water, and I am giving it to them. Call them lies if you please.'

" 'We still call them lies, but we understand.'

"We remained in that camp for over a week, and, in that period of time, we came to know what an important role the mullah played in this tribal community. People came to him with a variety of issues—property quarrels, marriage problems, thefts, suspicion of witchcraft, murders, or tribal disputes. Barrerai would drop into our camp every evening, and we learned that he was a widely traveled man and had lived with most of the border tribes at one time or another. Before we finally moved camp, he told us that he would be leaving that community after a few days. We were not overly surprised, because, from all he had told us about himself, we gathered he was a wanderer and needed a change now and then. This confirmed that he was not only an unusual person but more so an unusual tribal mullah, because any other would have been very reluctant to move once he had carved out a place and a secure livelihood for himself.

"Once we left the place, we forgot him completely. It was hardly likely that we would ever meet again, but strangely enough, our paths did cross, in fairly unusual circumstances. We had put our troops through a strenuous monthlong training exercise and decided that they deserved to relax. So it was arranged that a few sheep be slaughtered and an evening's entertainment be provided for the troops. Our commanding officer sent word to the nearby town, and a couple of days later, a small band of musicians together with singing boys and girls arrived at the fort. That evening, some time after we had retired to our rooms, a sudden commotion erupted in the camp, followed by a few rifle shots. We rushed out into the dark and found that a soldier had tried to assault one of the dancing girls, but the man in charge of the dancing party had come to her rescue. In the scuffle, the soldier opened fire with his rifle and hit the girl's protector in the shoulder.

"When I went to visit the wounded man in the hospital the next morning, who should I find but my old friend Mullah Barrerai? It was quite a surprise to find him, of all people, acting as the manager of dancing girls. Barrerai was not embarrassed in the least, and told me that he had done the job before, but never had it ended in the kind of violence he had experienced the previous night. He was all right, but he hoped that no harm would befall the girl. I assured him that the girls and the rest of the party were already on their way to town. At that, his mood lightened considerably, and he started to inquire about the prospects of getting employment with us. I told him that it was extremely doubtful, particularly as his popularity with the troops was bound to have suffered after the previous night's incident.

"I visited Mullah Barrerai regularly throughout his stay in the hospital. He was never very clear about his plans. Sometimes he would talk about going to the city for a while. Sometimes he would be critical of city life and would plan on going north, where he had not been for some years. He was a strangely disturbed man, and behind all his talk, one could sense an undertone of worry and fear, a feeling of failure. Indeed, he did mention on more than one occasion the virtues of a settled life, but he would immediately counter it by saying that he himself was not designed to live in one place permanently.

"One day, when I went to see him as usual, I learned that he had left suddenly and without telling anyone. I felt disappointed, but it was truly in character. He hated being tied down—whether it be to a place or to a person.

"Things had been quiet—in fact, unnaturally quiet—around our border posts and forts for some months. Even the usual sniping and cutting of telephone wires had ceased. This calm did not presage well, and worried us more than a little, because the Second World War had already started and any serious incident on our side of the border would embarrass the government considerably. We kept our ears close to the ground but could not discover anything brewing.

"One day, late in the evening, I received a message from one of the postern gates that a man wanted to see me on very urgent business. It was not unreasonable to suspect mischief, so we took all the necessary precautions before the gates were opened to admit the visitor. He was brought to me inside the guardroom. The stranger had wrapped the lower part of his face with the end of his turban. As the other people left the room, he revealed himself as a Wazir soldier who had deserted from one of our posts about a year ago.

" 'I have been sent by Mullah Barrerai,' he said. 'He

has ordered me to pass on to you a message. He says tell my friend, the captain, that there is great danger for him and his people, and he must take care.'

" 'Where does the danger come from, and how does Mullah Barrerai know of it?' I inquired.

" 'The danger comes from the Germans, your Farangi enemies. For a long time, they have been making payments, distributing arms and ammunition, and doling out promises through Mullah Barrerai. At their behest, he has been exciting them with the prospect of unlimited plunder on the plains and its people after the British lose their dominance. The situation is now ripe for starting a holy war against the British, and the trouble against you out here on the frontier could start any day.'

" 'If Mullah Barrerai calls himself my friend, how could he be party to this?'

" 'Why do you not understand? If it were not Mullah Barrerai, it would have been someone else. At least in him you have someone who may help you.'

"I thought this over for some time. 'Thank Mullah

Barrerai on my behalf. Thank him deeply for calling himself my friend,' I told my visitor. 'I would like to meet him.'

"'A meeting will be difficult but can be arranged later. In the meantime, I shall be in touch with you as his messenger.'

"I accompanied the messenger to the gate, where he was let out. I then hurried back to the mess to wake up the colonel. Our commanding officer was an old, experienced frontier campaigner who had originally served in the Irish Guards. But he'd opted for a transfer into the Indian army after his regiment was moved to England. He loved the area deeply, and had not once visited his hometown in Ireland in the past twenty years. After some discussion, he decided to send a telegram to the government, and at the same time to try and seek further confirmation of the truth or otherwise of the information brought to us.

"Before the next day was over, the information was fully confirmed. A whole company of Khassadars— native soldiers—deserted during the night with their weapons and ammunition. Most of the tribal chiefs and subchiefs who were due to visit the fort the next day to receive their six-monthly allowances failed to turn up. Instead, they sent representatives—usually distant relatives—to receive payments on their behalf.

"The period of uncertainty was now over. Our situation was indeed desperate. We were left with only a handful of troops on whose loyalty we could depend. The tribes of the area, together with their chiefs, were under the complete influence of our German enemy. We spent the next two days disarming the units of the tribal levies whose loyalty had become suspect, and in regrouping the troops left to us in strategic posts— abandoning the rest.

"The next evening the messenger from Mullah Barrerai visited us again. 'The mullah says,' he told us, 'that the tribes are now boiling with hatred. They are gathering from far and wide to share in the German money and loot, and to take part in what they are calling a religious war. He says that the talk of money and of religion has excited them to the point where everybody has abandoned you. He says that once fighting starts, he will not be able to stop it, and you have only one chance.'

" 'What chance does he give us?' I inquired.

" 'He says that you will have to match money with money, and it is a risk worth taking, because money will be of no use to you if your forts and posts are overrun. He says that if you are willing to trust him, you should go to him openly with as much money as you can collect, but it should in no case be less than fifty thousand gold sovereigns.'

"I made the visitor wait while I hurried to the colonel and gave him the news. The colonel smiled as I finished the story.

" 'I knew it would come to that,' he said, 'and I have already obtained the approval of the government to do what you suggest. You have my permission to negotiate with the rebels.'

"I returned to the messenger and told him that I would be visiting their camp the next day with some soldiers, and that I would be carrying money with me.

I was confident that I would be safe from them, but wanted to make sure that my escort was also covered by their safe conduct. Just before the messenger left, he again repeated, 'The mullah wanted to make clear to you that you must bring the money openly and make no secret of the amount.'

" 'I will do as he says, though I do not understand the reason behind it.'

"Fifty thousand gold sovereigns is no light weight, and we had to pack it on four mules. These, together with my escort and myself mounted on horses, made our small party look quite impressive as we left the fort at first light the next morning. By midday, we reached the camp of the hostiles, where Mullah Barrerai was waiting for us. He was surrounded by more than a score of his lieutenants, some of whom had been on our side till very recently. The whole area was full of small encampments where thousands of tribesmen had gathered over the past days, preparing for an attack against our forts. Mullah Barrerai gave no sign of recognition as we met him.

"As soon as lunch was over, Mullah Barrerai collected the key leaders among the tribesmen and addressed them in our presence. What he told them briefly was that of the two reasons that were being given for the gathering of the tribes against the British government, one was religion, and the other was money. As far as religion was concerned, it was a false argument, because the Germans were also nonbelievers, and their religion was no different from what the British professed.

"As far as money was concerned, the Germans had given some money, but mostly it was promises, and the worth of a German promise had never been tested so far. As against this, from the British side, a representative was now with them, carrying gold, and prepared to match each German promise with cash. So what would they choose?

"It appeared that Barrerai had been talking to these people in the same strain for some time past. Our arrival with packs of gold clearly tilted popular opinion in our favor, and before the afternoon was over, the tribes solemnly decided to accept the payment offered by the British and to disperse after returning the arms that the deserters had taken away. He beckoned for me to move nearer.

" 'Are you happy at the outcome?' he asked in a low voice.

" 'I don't know whether to be happy,' I replied. 'Now that the tribes have smelled money, what happens if they get a bigger offer from the Germans tomorrow or think we have more to offer?'

"Barrerai's face broke into his old familiar smile. 'Ah, you do not understand. If payment were to be made, you would indeed be in deep trouble. Payment is not going to be made. This night, you and I and the money are going to disappear. Do you understand what it would mean?'

" 'Tell me!'

" 'When this happens, they will lose the only person they have considered honest enough to trust with money. There will be so much suspicion and bitterness that they will never again be able to gather under one banner. So you will secure both your safety and your money. Do you now understand what is in my mind?'

" 'I do now. This can work beautifully, but what is going to happen to you? You must take some money before you go.'

" 'Friend, taking money from you would be like eating pig meat. Do not ever mention this again. I can always find a living.'

" 'But this time you do not understand. If we do what you suggest, you can never be the same person as you were in the past. You will be hunted, because men will suspect you of carrying a fortune on yourself, and they will be seeking you in revenge for stealing their share of gold.'

" 'This is of no importance,' he insisted. 'I have always lived with a little trouble of one kind or another. I know that as a friend you would do the same for me.'

"With that, he refused to discuss the subject any further. He remained silent not only during the few hours we stayed on in the camp, but even as we left for the fort during the middle of the night.

"I don't even know when he left the party. One moment he was there, and the next he was gone. He must have quietly slipped away on the mule he was riding. It was typical of him to leave without fuss and without saying good-bye."

After a pause, the old Scouts officer once again turned to the Malik of the Bhittanis. "You have heard the story now. Do you not wonder at the generosity which lay within his breast? Can you now understand why I am impelled to visit his grave and pray for his spirit, and why I consider any insult to his memory so unjust?"

The Bhittani chief pondered for a while before replying. "Friend," he said, "Mullah Barrerai shall ever remain to all of us a dishonest rogue who cheated us out of our due. He made free with what was not his to give. His whim brought sorrow to a large number of men. His crime is no less if he did it out of friendship for you. So let us talk about him no more." He took the officer by the arm. "Come, have some tea before you leave."

Five

A KIDNAPPING

A thin trickle of water flowing down the Shaktu River demarcates the boundary between the Wazirs and the Mahsuds—the two predatory tribes of Waziristan. On either side of the river are narrow vestigial banks where Wazir and Mahsud women look after ragged patches of corn. The river provides only a brief inter-ruption. Where the fields end, the convolutions and whorls of bare, cruel rock once again resume their march across the land—occasionally throwing up spires and lances of granite into the sky.

For the greater part of the year, the Mahsud and the

Wazir glower at each other from across the distance that separates the two: Mahsuds from their cluster of squat houses with narrow slit-like windows, and Wazirs from the tops of the towers that protect each home. Every few months, their hate and tensions explode into violence and some men die, never the women, who continue caring for the land and fetching water from the river. After a few days of violence, the caretakers of a small shrine near the bed of the river walk out and arrange a truce to last for the next few months, until the silence is once again broken by rifle shots.

The Mahsuds, because they always hunt in groups, are known as the wolves of Waziristan. A Wazir hunts alone. He is known as "the leopard" to other men. Despite their differences, the two tribes share more than merely their common heritage of poverty and misery. Nature has bred in both an unusual abundance of anger, enormous resilience, and a total refusal to accept their fate. If nature provides them food for only ten days in a year, they believe in their right to demand the rest of their sustenance from their fellow men who live oily, fat, and comfortable lives in the plains. To both tribes, survival is the ultimate virtue. In neither community is any stigma attached to a hired assassin, a thief, a kidnapper, or an informer. And then, both are totally absorbed in themselves. They have no doubt in their minds that they occupy center stage, while the rest of the world acts out minor roles or watches them as spectators—as befit inferior species.

Winter was late that year. It was already the end of November, and the men from the Waziristan hills were watching the slow and leisurely change in season with growing impatience. They felt cheated, because a short winter meant much less time for gathering their sustenance for the year. They knew—as did the people of the plains—that winter was the time of raids, kidnappings, and robberies. These long, cold nights that made people huddle in heavy quilts also made them reluctant and slow in reacting to a neighbor's cry for help. There was also very little movement at night, unlike in summer, when one was likely to come across men wandering in the fields at any time, engaged in watering their lands. And, too, the winter nights were long enough to permit a safe retreat into the hills before the dawn broke.

In the houses sprinkled around the Shaktu Valley in Waziristan, three men were turning over in their minds the idea of leading a kidnapping raid into a cantonment about ten miles away from the foot of the hills. Each of the men was aware of what the others were thinking. The first, Sarmast Khan, a Mahsud, was about thirty years old. It was his ventures over the past fifteen years that had provided the necessary capital for the firewood business set up by his two brothers in Karachi. This time, he was in need of money for himself. The father of the girl betrothed to him had been pressing for payment of the balance of the bride price.

In a small house a few miles away, twin brothers, thirty-two years old and from the Wazir tribe, needed money for another reason. Since their first crime, the theft of a beautiful engraved rifle from an official traveling on a government road fifteen years ago, they had accumulated a long record of offenses in the lower districts where their families lived. What this meant was that while they were free to roam the hills, where no policemen would go after them, they were hunted men in the plains.

Now, at last, the twins had been offered a chance to start new lives. A senior officer of the nearest district had agreed to their unconditional surrender, and in return had promised to pardon their past offenses. However, the file had been sent to the government, where a clerk had sent word that their case would go through only on payment of a two-thousand-rupee bribe. The two brothers were placed, therefore, in the ironic position of having to commit one final raid to steal enough money to enable them to start honest lives.

While these men were brooding, other men were similarly worried about how they would spend the coming winter. Sarmast and the twin brothers, Jalat

Khan and Zabta Khan, met one morning after the women of the village had left to fetch the day's drinking water. There was considerable agreement among them as to the basic arrangements. They agreed on the choice of the leader—Daulat Khan, also a Mahsud, a grizzled old veteran who was known throughout the tribal areas for his broad humor, his predilection for stories, and the hearing aid he wore, which he had stolen from a farmer some years ago. They were also of one mind about who would keep the person they kidnapped, and who would negotiate the ransom payment.

They decided that the party would, tentatively, comprise ten persons, including themselves. On this basis, the ransom would have to be divided into thirteen shares, with one extra share each for the leader, the negotiator, and the person who provided food, shelter, and information in the city. They also agreed that their group must include at least two men from the Bhittanis—the tribe through whose lands they would have to pass on their mission.

It was late in the afternoon, and the deputy commissioner of Bannu was winding up the day's work and wondering whether he could get in a set or two of tennis before dark. There had been a particularly heavy rush of visitors that day, of whom about half a dozen still remained. Of these, one was particularly important—an informer who had brought in useful snippets of information on a few occasions. There he sat, on a wooden bench outside the office—a stocky-looking young man with a beard, his eyes darkened with kohl, wearing a red secondhand ladies' overcoat with a fur collar.

This garment, which might at one time have been the pride of the wardrobe of a suburban American housewife, was unbuttoned. The ivory shafts of two daggers were clearly visible, thrust into the waistband of his trousers.

The deputy commissioner called in a couple more visitors before the informer was invited into the office.

It was necessary to keep him waiting for his turn, as any special treatment would be immediately noticed and become the subject of bazaar gossip. It would also demonstrate the anxiety of the officer, placing the informer at a psychological advantage. The selling of information was far from a dishonorable way of earning one's livelihood, and no informer in these parts made a secret of his profession. One such person had even erected an arch to welcome a touring official, with a banner proudly proclaiming that it had been put up by a "spy in the service of the government."

Some families had been in the information trade for generations. And most of the informers were not owned by one master. They retailed information to whosoever was willing to buy it. They would even sell the same information to more than one person. The more clients an informer had, the better respected he was by his peers.

Tor Baz was, however, a newcomer in the field. He entered the room after taking off his shoes as a mark of respect for the officer, moved toward the lone electric heater, which provided the only warmth in the chilly room, sat down next to it, and started warming his hands and feet while cracking his knuckles. After a while, he looked toward the deputy commissioner, who sat watching him patiently.

"Are you strong, sahib?"

"Are you happy?" responded the officer.

"Are you happy, sahib?" replied the informer.

"Are you well, Tor Baz?" queried the deputy commissioner.

"Are things well in your family, deputy commissioner sahib?"

"Yes," came the reply patiently. "The blessings of God are with us."

With this exchange of salutations completed, an essential and inescapable part of any meeting, both men sat quietly for a while, each waiting for the other to speak first. At last Tor Baz accepted defeat and tentatively remarked, "There are strange doings and happenings beyond your border, sahib."

"A dependable man alone makes a good friend, Tor Baz," he said. "Tell me all that your eyes have seen."

"It is for this that I have come to see you," Tor Baz remarked. "There is a kidnapping gang heading toward this area. Last evening, I myself saw a collection of twenty men at a hamlet of Tori Khel Wazirs. They were led by Daulat Khan, and here is a list of the persons I could identify. There were four persons who were complete strangers to me."

The deputy commissioner was watching the expression flitting across the face of the informer as he told his tale. He would have preferred at least two more versions of the story before making up his mind, but since there was no immediate likelihood of more informers turning up that late in the day, he would have to deduce the facts the best he could from the material made available to him.

To start with, he accepted the fact that a gang had been formed in the hills and was heading for his district. In fact, gangs were already overdue this late in the season. Kidnappings usually started in October, with the onset of winter, but it was already late November, and no kidnappings had been reported.

The number of people in the gang was, of course, exaggerated, as a large gang was formed only for hold-ups on the roads. He doubted whether any man in his right mind would plan a holdup on the roads in winter, when the district could be sealed tight with check-points at the few roads free of ice and snow. He reflected for a while on the information.

"Tor Baz," he asked, "where would they find the targets? At night, families huddle together for warmth. During the day, the traffic is very light. The winter makes it difficult for the kidnappers to scurry back into the hills as fast as they would like to. You know the city dwellers will slow them down."

"The paths may be icy, the springs frozen, the hostages lethargic and obese, but the men from the hills, although equipped only with patched shoes, will manage to get them into the hills before they are checked. Once embarked on this venture, the gang will not be deterred, even if rain and snow makes walking difficult."

The deputy commissioner caught the hint and

counted out forty rupees for a new pair of shoes and another twenty for the expenses of the journey. The scene drew to a conclusion, as always, with Tor Baz expressing great indignation and then reluctantly accepting the payment when the deputy commissioner told him that he would be deeply hurt if Tor Baz refused it.

As Tor Baz turned to leave, the deputy commissioner's voice stopped him: "Tor Baz," he said reflectively, "tell me one thing. Who are you? You live with the Wazirs, but you are not one of them. With your looks, you could be taken for a Mahsud, which you are not, because your accent and your way of speaking are different. I have been trying to place you, but I have failed. Who are you, and where do you come from?"

Tor Baz's hands went to his heavy woolen cap, on which a small silver amulet had been stitched. He pulled the cap off and started twisting it in his strong hands. As he removed the cap, his jet-black hair and the shaved nape of his neck showed clearly in the fluorescent light of the room.

"Sahib," he spoke after a while, "you have asked me a question I have not been asked for a long time now." His eyes started crinkling, and all of a sudden he was laughing. Heavy, gusty laughter filled the room. Then he spoke: "It is true, I am neither a Mahsud nor a Wazir. But I can tell you as little about who I am as I can about who I shall be. Think of Tor Baz as your hunting falcon. That should be enough."

As Tor Baz closed the door of the office behind him, the deputy commissioner heard him loudly spit on the veranda floor.

The gang was already in town. In fact, they had been there for more than twenty-four hours and had spent most of this time checking on the various choices of victims available. The owner of a tobacco warehouse had been rejected as a prospective prize because there were too many women in his household. One of the gang members had scouted the house and informed them that the women were in the habit of chattering till the early hours of the morning. Another good target had to be abandoned because there were too many lights around the house; another because the man was a tribesman himself. Finally, they agreed on a group of schoolteachers, six in number, who lived by themselves in one of the rooms of a school building.

Schoolteachers, doctors, and street cleaners were always attractive targets for kidnappings. These groups went on strikes so promptly after every kidnapping that the ransom was usually quickly forthcoming from one quarter or another, even if the relatives of the men did not or could not pay up.

It was well after dawn when the excited superintendent of police telephoned the deputy commissioner and informed him that six schoolteachers appeared to have been kidnapped during the night from a room in which they had been sleeping. The door had been broken open, and there were signs of a struggle. The rest of the story was familiar. The people in the hundreds of houses around claimed to have heard no dogs bark, no sounds of the building being broken into, nor sounds of any struggle or calls for help. The people had kept quiet during the night but were making up for it now, when they were sure that they were safe. There were loud recriminations against the police for not protecting them, protestations at being treated like women by the tribesmen, demands for arming them at government expense with weapons deadly enough to counter the marauding tribesmen—the usual cacophony that followed the descent of hill men into the plains.

The officials were informed, and they calmed the people by explaining to them that the response to the crime would be according to the law and the procedures laid down a century ago, which were as effective then as they were today.

The relationship between the tribes and the government was based on a formal treaty entered into by two contracting parties. The treaty stipulated in precise terms the payment of a regular yearly stipend to the tribe and noninterference in their customs and management of their affairs. The obligation on the part of the tribes was the good conduct of each member of their community and of those residing in their area of responsibility. This was formally termed as "collective tribal and territorial responsibility." The tribe or its members could be chastened for any lapse or infraction in this responsibility through the authority of an instrument called the Frontier Crimes Regulations. Punishment could range from detention of any member of the tribe, whether or not directly responsible, to the institution of a blockade and even suspension of the yearly payment. The ultimate punishment was a punitive expedition by the government.

Orders were issued to set in motion the first response under the Frontier Crimes Regulations. The men of law were called on to comb the bazaars, to spot any Tori Khel Wazirs and pick them up, to seal their shops and confiscate any vehicle owned by their tribe. This action would, it was hoped, provide a counter-pressure, and would persuade the tribe to release the hostages.

Such action was most effective if a close relative of the kidnappers was caught, which was not likely. They would make sure to stay away from the area for some days. The captives would now be released under only two circumstances: either the ransom was paid, or the district officials and the relatives of the hostages were prepared to remain indifferent to their fate, to the point of establishing that no ransom would ever be paid. The latter attitude, which demanded patience of the highest degree, was easier for a tribesman than it was for a city dweller. Therefore, there appeared to be a very fair prospect for a sizable return to the men of the winter's first gang.

The tracking party, led by a young assistant commissioner, followed the tracks up to the border of the district where the tribal area began. In their path lay the Bhittani tribe. They halted there for a while and sent some men to summon the *jirga* of that tribe, an assembly of elders and leaders. After a few hours, the *jirga* assembled and sat down on their side of the boundary line. This was not merely a point of honor, it was also a mark of caution—for once they stepped across the boundary, they would become subject to the laws of the settled district and could be arrested by the police—a thought that was anathema to every tribesman. When the *jirga* had assembled, the assistant commissioner got up and addressed them formally.

"Elders and graybeards of the Bhittani tribe," he said, "an offense has been committed in your neighboring district. During the night, a gang of outlaws has kidnapped some schoolteachers from a village a few miles away and has taken them by force. All the signs and the reading of the tracks prove to us that this gang, both while moving into the district and also while escaping, did so through your area. As proof, we can show you the trail which we have followed, right to the edge of your territory."

He paused for a while and then continued: "You are familiar with the treaties between you and us. Under the terms of the treaty, not only is a tribe responsible for the action of its people but it is also responsible for any act which takes place in its area or through its area. This, of course, is apart from the stigma on your honor, which such an act is bound to attract. I, therefore, call on you to accept this responsibility. I require of you to apprehend and surrender the outlaws and the captives. If you fail in this, you would be considered by us as having broken our agreement and shall be responsible for the consequences."

As the assistant commissioner finished, a heavy murmur arose from the assembled *jirga*. They realized that they were indeed in a fix. The terms of the treaty were clear enough, and yet theirs was a small tribe that could not conceivably take upon itself the task of forcing the Mahsuds, of all people, to return the captives or to surrender the accused.

After talking among themselves for a while, they signaled that their reply was ready. When the men had quieted down, an old Bhittani tribesman—the most senior of all the elders present—got up with the help of a long wooden staff that had small studs hammered into it as decoration.

"Sahib," he started off in a thin, quivering voice, "you are right. The treaties are clear enough, as also is our obligation under them. Indeed, we are deeply impressed that you, who look so young and tender in years, should have taken so much pain and spent so much labor in studying them."

He stopped and let his glance rest on the upturned faces around him. There was a gleam of triumph in his eyes at the quip he had just made against the young official. This was immediately appreciated by his audience, which chuckled and grinned openly. The officer flushed with anger and embarrassment.

"Sahib, we also acknowledge the shame brought upon our tribe by the outlaws who used our land to seek access to your area. It is indeed a terrible insult to us. But"—he paused again before adding—"let me narrate to you a story."

The crowd went silent, listening intently to the old man's voice, which had now become clear and sharp, like the sound of plucked strings from a musical instrument.

"The story goes, sahib, that a young boy and girl eloped and were running away from their homes, when they suddenly found themselves surrounded by a pack of ruffians out for mischief. These rascals, men of no honor, surrounded the couple and, threatening them with death, dishonored the girl. Not finding enough satisfaction in it, they asked the young man to strip and had their sport with him. After doing all this, these terrible and wicked fellows left the couple and went away. As their oppressors disappeared, the young man and girl calmed themselves and put on their clothes. The young man, after his fear had died, became furious with the girl. He accused her of having proven untrustworthy, disloyal, and faithless. He also charged her with possessing no sense of shame or modesty, as she had let so many men violate her body.

"The girl thought for a while. Then she squared her shoulders, looked at the young man, and replied. Do you know what answer she gave him?"

"Tell us, tell us," cried the audience, spellbound by the story.

"Well, the girl spoke thus: 'My love,' she said, 'you are right. My body has been violated, but think of one thing. My body has been fashioned by nature for this very purpose. What was done to me was indeed wrong, but truly speaking, it is, as it were, only what nature has intended for me when it created me. Now look at yourself, you are a man. You were not made to be used the way these rascals used you. Yet you did not resist them. You allowed yourself to be violated just as I did. What reason do you offer?'"

The old man stopped to let the effect of his story sink in before he continued: "So, officer sahib, that is what we say to you. We, the Bhittanis, are a weak tribe as compared to the Mahsuds. Yet nature has placed us on their borders. Because of this, the Mahsuds have to use our land when they go out of theirs or cross back into it. We do not like it but cannot stop them. We do not have the force that they command.

"But what about you? What about all your police and your people in the districts who allow themselves to be kidnapped? You are like the man in the story. What the Mahsuds do to you, and the impunity with which they do it, was not intended by nature. Your nature should compel you to see that such things do not happen. Yet you let them do it, and when the deed is done, you rush out and vent your fury on others."

The old man's story and its irrefutable logic had the whole assembly rolling with laughter. Even the police party and the group of officials from the district could not resist, and they, too, joined in the hilarity.

Only the young officer stood crestfallen, realizing that he had performed poorly in his first battle of wits with the tribesmen. He could offer no story to counter the old man's logic, and therefore his own case, though it had appeared to rest on such a sure and solid foundation, now stood demolished. There was no option available to him for the moment but to gracefully accept defeat. He hoped that his colleagues would not hear of the story.

On approaching the hills, the band of men rested for a while near the spring. They baked bread and shared it with their captives, and also arranged for a few mules to carry the footsore teachers the rest of the way. Their destination was the house of an old man, Mandos, who was going to care for the captives and negotiate their ransom in return for a share of the proceeds. They reached the house after dark and found the old man finishing his midnight prayers. A room had been prepared for the captives. Since such a large number had not been expected, quilts had to be shared, two men to one quilt.

When the morning came, one of the schoolteachers was asked to write a letter addressed to his relatives, indicating their fair state of health and the name of their host, and including, most important of all, fervent pleas for meeting the terms of their kidnappers and securing their early release. They were then served a breakfast of fried chicken, wheat cakes, and tea. From now on until their release, the hostages would be looked after with greater care and diligence than a tribesman can spare for his own sons.

On the second day after the kidnapping, the deputy commissioner received the information that the party had crossed into Waziristan and was heading toward Mandos's safe house in the notorious Shaktu Valley, which had provided sanctuary for half a century to most of the outlaws in the area. The fact that Mandos's name had come to the forefront so early established quite clearly that this old man would do the *yagh*—make the proclamation about the terms for release of the captives from his custody.

The large, mountainous territory of Waziristan was split into two administrative units, each with a political agent in charge. The two political agents were informed of the news, because from now on the game would have to be played by them and their people. Regular laws did not apply here, and the Frontier Crimes Regulations were the primary instrument of administration with which they had to try to balance the needs and customs of the tribes with the commands that reached them from the government.

The political agent of North Waziristan was head-quartered in a fort at Miranshah. The political agent of South Waziristan, who dealt mainly with the

Mahsuds, had his base in a small cantonment at a place called Wana. These bases had not changed much in the past fifty years. Most of the men lived without their families, bugles were still blown in the morning, and the retreat formally sounded in the evening. The pickets and outposts retained their old British names—Guides Hill, Gordon Hill, Gibraltar Picket— as did the roads in the cantonment and the gates of Miranshah Fort.

One of the few recent changes was that the two political agents could now communicate with each other by wireless. And it was over wireless that they agreed on the arrangements for handling the problem. As the first step, they had decided that since Mandos was a Mahsud, the Mahsud chiefs and elders would be collected and required to proceed to the Shaktu Valley to bring back the hostages, while a similar group from among the Wazirs would be sent to make sure that Mandos did not, as one likely gambit, move the captives into Wazir territory.

The Mahsud *jirga* was in tremendous spirits. The

next few days would be a kind of vacation for them, with long parleys and the sharing of jokes and stories at the expense of the government. For a few days, there would be no worries about families. Instead, desultory bargaining about the ransom for the hostages was interspersed with lengthy discussion about diverse subjects, such as the safest smuggling routes, the most profitable items of contraband, the relative quality of weaponry currently available in the market, the rising prices of ammunition, and all the current social gossip and scandals in the area.

The *jirga* had taken eighteen thousand rupees in cash along with them. This was known to the gang even before their arrival. The bargaining continued for three days before an agreement was reached at twenty thousand rupees. After the deal was finalized, Daulat Khan, the head of the kidnapping party, graciously reduced the amount by another two thousand rupees as a gesture of hospitality to the *jirga* of his tribe.

The money and the captives changed hands, and yet another Waziristan kidnapping case was closed.

Six

THE GUIDE

> *If the ears of my corn be empty, let them stand as high as those of my rival.*
>
> —Afridi proverb

For more than a quarter of a century, the thought of undertaking this journey had dominated my life in one way or another. For the first few years, my father and I had dreamed about it together. He talked of returning to the land of his birth, and I reveled in the thought of missing the drab school days in the small German village school I was enrolled in, wandering away, seeking adventure in the company of my father. But reality was harsher. These were years of poverty, when my parents had to virtually break their backs in eking out enough sustenance from the small farm in Bavaria that my mother had inherited. Then came the war, and all our hopes had to be set aside. When the war ended, my father died and I was left alone to nurse our dreams and nourish them, year after year, as time passed and the journey had to be postponed. Finally, after years of frustration, there came a time when fortune, instead of conspiring against me, as it had seemed to, started to favor me, and I grabbed the opportunity to make the trip.

Once I had made the decision, I took careful stock of my limitations. My knowledge of Pashto, never as good as my father wanted, had grown even rustier with disuse after his death. Though I had tried to practice it during the few months I had spent in Kabul as the representative of my firm, I lacked the confidence to speak freely and naturally in this language. What also loomed in my mind was the harsh fact that Tirah was a land forbidden to anybody other than true Afridis, and anyone who violated this unwritten injunction would be in serious danger. Similarly, in spite of my efforts, the clothes of my father's people—loose gray-colored cotton trousers, a long shirt, a waistcoat, and black blanket over my shoulders, and sandals of raw untanned leather on my feet—felt uncomfortable and alien. I felt like a foreigner. My only advantage lay in the fact that some friends had recommended to me two guides, on whose loyalty and steadfastness I could depend.

The three of us entered the larger of the two rooms of the hut, which lay only a few miles from the point where we crossed into the Afridi area, leaving our host, Gul Zarin, outside, as he'd expected us to. The distant glow from the city of Peshawar was still visible. We had decided on an early halt to refresh ourselves so as to start before dawn the next day. As we sat down on our cots, one of my companions turned to the other.

"Gul Zarin is asking too many questions," he remarked. His companion nodded slowly.

"Perhaps it would be better to silence him." They both turned to look at me.

"No, no," came my quick reply. "He is only being curious because I have given him reason to be so. He means no harm."

My vehemence surprised my companions. They talked for a while longer in whispers. Early the next morning, we made the expected payment to Gul Zarin for his hospitality and started off. The stars were still bright and clear, and the mist had not yet started rising from the ground. The air was extremely cold, and our breath and that of our animals froze into vapor as we continued climbing to the top of the range, beyond which lay the homeland of the Afridis.

After traveling for a mile or so, one of the guides slipped away for a while, anxious about any danger lurking along the trail ahead. We took more than two hours, by my reckoning, to reach the top of the last ridge. Shortly after we started, the previous day's pain returned and I had to rest frequently until my breathing became less labored and my leg muscles relaxed somewhat. Whenever we halted, my companions made obvious efforts to make me feel less embarrassed than I did, courteously pretending that they, too, needed the rest. At these times, Hamesh Gul, who was an Afridi himself, would move a little ahead and sit hunched over his rifle while the other, the man who called himself Tor Baz, would remain with me, sometimes tending to my blisters, sometimes giving me a few gulps of water out of the goatskin bag tied on to one of the mules. They could not, hard as they tried, hide their nervousness at these halts.

While we walked, Hamesh Gul talked to me about his people, the Afridis. When he talked of them, he didn't speak of them as just one of the many tribes living in this harsh borderland between Pakistan and Afghanistan. There was a total assurance in his voice, and a belief that the Afridis were the only people who mattered. The other tribes merely provided the setting for the Afridi jewel to shine and display its brilliance.

I had expected an angry denial from our other companion, but to my surprise, I found Tor Baz agreeing with Hamesh Gul.

He explained the ancient division of the tribe into the eight famous clans, each proud and independent. Occasionally, when the need arose, they joined together in various combinations to act in concert. He spoke with pride of the tribe's fights with the British, out of which they had emerged with honor and, at the same time, with respect and affection for their adversaries. Interspersed with this detailed account—some of it extremely confusing to me—were descriptions of a few tribal raids on the city people. The Afridis, he claimed, with a perceptible squaring of his shoulders, had regularly raided Peshawar, and the very name of their tribe had inspired terror in this large city, whose traders had made it one of the richest in Central Asia. He claimed that his tribe had denied passage to all the conquerors of the Indian subcontinent through the famous Khyber Pass, permitting the raiders through only after they had paid for the privilege in cash.

When I reached the crest of the last hilltop, my companions were waiting for me. They had moved away from the track to a small bald patch that lay amid thick pine forests for miles around.

The sun had come out about half an hour before. It was still weak, but the sunshine was gradually driving out the effects of last night's drizzle from our bodies and from the foliage around us. With the rising sun, my sores and bug bites, mementos of my host's quilt of the previous evening, started itching furiously.

I stood on a flat rock and watched the panorama that stretched out before me. There, resting like a saucer-shaped depression within the ring of dark, forbidding mountains, was Maidan, the heart of Tirah, the land of a quarter of a million or more Afridis. Standing at this height, one could look over its entire expanse, about fifty square miles of it. It seemed from this distance like a neat patchwork quilt of green colors interspersed with tiny stones and mud houses, each with a tower.

"And there"—Hamesh Gul pointed at a sparkle of

lights from a tin roof right in the center of the depression—"that is Bagh—our capital."

I was home at last. The tenuous link that had been created by my dead father and nurtured all these years by my memory of his lonely and sad living years had finally brought me to the land of his people.

"I am an Afridi, too, you know," I told Hamesh Gul.

"Where from?" he inquired.

"From the Upper Qamber Khels," I replied, and explained my background to him.

"If you have remained away for all these years, your cousins must have captured your fields. I hope they do not find your return irksome. Shall we start out now?"

The word "cousin" in my father's language meant both a family relationship and one's bitter enemy. If I had thought to impress him with the romance in the story, I had failed. His matter-of-fact acceptance of the reasons for my journey nettled me. Perhaps to him, there was nothing strange about an Afridi—even a half-Afridi—visiting his homeland. Perhaps such a compulsion was to be taken for granted. I half began to understand the intensity of feeling that had rent my father's heart at his inability to move back among his people.

"Yes, I am ready to move now," I told my companions. Tor Baz hit the front mule with a switch, and we started on our downward journey. It was quite a relief to be traveling downhill; my legs, which had been silently protesting at going uphill, now suddenly felt relaxed at this unexpected relief. I was also helped considerably by a thick staff that Tor Baz had fashioned for me out of an oak sapling. With walking becoming easier, I found it possible to take greater interest in the surroundings than I had done in the last two days.

The day had finally dawned. Soon we were meeting groups of people. A few girls walked past with water pitchers on their heads to fetch water from some spring, perhaps miles away. They would make at least three trips during the day to get water for their menfolk, and yet find it within themselves to make another trip to refill the wayside casks that provided water for travelers. They were talking brightly among themselves, but their chatter fell silent as they approached the party of strangers. In this land where imputation of immorality meant certain death, both men and women were careful.

We saw a long string of ponies winding their way at a lower level; they had been loaded with fine timber. Some were loaded with hand-cut logs, but mostly they transported trunks of young pine trees stripped of their bark, to be sold in the cities for the frames of string cots.

The track wound its way over bare outcrops of rock. While still descending, we came across many and various signs of human habitation. We met parties of firewood collectors. These were usually small bands of women and girls who moved exceedingly fast so they could reach and occupy the best sites before the others did. The matrons walked in front, while the very young girls—some of them hardly eight or nine years old—skipped along in the rear. Apart from carrying cutting tools, each had her own water bottle (usually an old army issue) and a small inconspicuous bundle, which contained the day's food. They rushed past us almost in a flash, without sparing even a glance for any of us. They appeared completely absorbed by their immediate quest—to seek out and establish them-selves in favorable grounds before the rush began.

We crossed small flocks of animals—sheep and goats and sometimes a few cows. They were herded by young boys and girls, who also carried water bottles and food. Whenever they passed us, one of them would give a whack to the nearest animal—a gesture of defiance or bravado, perhaps in unconscious imita-tion of the grown-ups.

Soon fields began to appear. The first one was just a patch, hardly bigger than two beds placed end to end. It rested by itself, a lonely and pathetic spot of green among giant boulders and rocks. Its owner, whoever he was, for no house was in sight, had carefully con-structed a high wall of stones around it to prevent years of hard work from being destroyed by a vagrant flood.

More fields came in sight, and also the first houses. Squat buildings with thick walls made out of small round boulders set in mud, half buried in the ground. No-nonsense houses without embellishments of any sort, meant for protection from the weather and designed to be defended against sudden assault.

It was midday, and we were still in the Kuki Khel area—belonging to the second-largest of the Afridi clans. Hamesh Gul, who was leading, turned us away from the main track.

"We shall go to my father-in-law's house," he explained. "The old man is a trusted *malik* of the government and is usually in Peshawar in Pakistan. His wife lives in the mountains." Hamesh Gul had himself served the Afghanistan government and had received an allowance from them. It could as easily have been the other way around, as long as the other government was willing to pay for the privilege.

Soon we reached a house, and Hamesh Gul stood a short distance away, cupped his hands, and shouted, "Is anybody home in Amir Khan's house?"

After a few moments, a face half showed itself in one of the slits in the wall that served as a window.

"Who is it, wanting to know?" a woman's voice shouted back.

"It is I, Hamesh Gul, Amir Khan's son-in-law."

"Which daughter of mine have you married?" the disembodied voice called back skeptically.

"The one after the eldest. I have brought two guests."

After a minute or two, the door was unlatched and an old woman beckoned us inside. We tied the mules outside. As we entered, she caught Hamesh Gul by his sleeve.

"How is my daughter?" she asked.

"She is well," he replied. "I will ask her to look you up."

It was not until later that I came to know that Hamesh Gul had never visited his in-laws, nor had the old woman seen her daughter after the marriage. That was now more than twenty years ago.

The old woman shuffled about inside, making preparations for her guests. It had required no offer on her part, and no polite demureness on ours, for her to start preparing food. There were no shops and no restaurants, and any travelers—even strangers—had to be fed.

While the food was being prepared, Hamesh Gul talked about the clan he had married into. The Kuki Khels were the second-largest of the eight clans. Law-abiding and peaceful, their greatest moment had been when their chief had been recognized as the chief of all the Afridis by the British. Their second venture into prominence had also come through the same family, when one of the sons had raised the standard of revolt against the Pakistani government. As a result, their castle (we were to see this imposing structure later) had been bombed by the Pakistani air force, and there it stood to this day—a blackened empty shell. The son had obstinately argued that since the government had damaged the building, it was for them to repair it.

As the old woman brought in the food—some coarse millet loaves, a chicken cooked with lentils, and a jug of sour buttermilk—Hamesh Gul turned to her and said, "Can we have some walnuts and corncobs to eat on the way?"

The old woman's distress and anger were plain to us. Very reluctantly, she went away to fetch them. Hamesh Gul gave a chuckle. "These Kuki Khels have the sweetest corn and walnuts in the world and hate parting with them," he explained. "She cannot refuse them today, because that would be an insult to guests. I knew I would get some off her." He chuckled deeply again, and Tor Baz joined in the mirth.

The food over, we took leave, Hamesh Gul tarrying a little, his bundle of corncobs and walnuts hanging over his shoulders. "I will send your daughter to you," he promised. "Do you want to send some corncobs for her?"

"She should grow her own," the old woman retorted savagely, and turned her back on us.

Hamesh Gul was still laughing when a rifle shot rang out. It hit the door that had just closed behind us. Within a minute, the old woman fired back defiantly from her house.

I had stopped in confusion. "Don't worry," said Hamesh Gul, continuing to laugh. "These two families have been feuding with each other for the last two generations. The men from both houses are away, but the old women let loose at each other once in a while."

We now started hurrying toward our destination. Where our pace had been slow and leisurely for the last two days, Hamesh Gul insisted on our crossing into the Qamber Khel area before dusk so that he did not have to spend a night in alien territory. When the pace started telling on me, they simply placed me on one of the pack animals, fashioned two rough stirrups, and rushed along, almost without a pause. I could not understand the reason for their haste, but it was explained to me later.

Hamesh Gul's mother-in-law had slipped him a word of warning that some trouble was expected between her clan and their neighbors; that the Kuki Khels might try to lay ambushes on the tracks leading through their area to deny passage to their enemies. Whenever this happened, movement between the two areas would be totally suspended until the elders or the mullahs of both tribes arrived at some agreement.

The boundary between the tribes was not marked in any way. But suddenly, in the middle of a path, while we were following a gushing stream, Hamesh Gul relaxed and became solicitous about my welfare. He insisted on my getting down and resting. He asked me to cup my hands and take a drink of water from a trickling spring. "The sweetest water in the world," he said. He laughed and joked with two small boys fishing in midstream, and as a final sign of his relaxation, he picked some wild pomegranate flowers from a tree and stuck them carefully on his cap. He wished he could buy a transistor radio. "It makes one forget one's tiredness," he claimed.

"Of course, I could not have dared to mention it only ten years ago," he said, and laughed. "The poor man who brought the first radio to Tirah was hauled up before the mullahs. His transistor was condemned, and a firing squad shot it to bits."

Hamesh Gul left Tor Baz and me to walk at a slow pace and hurried ahead to make arrangements for the night's lodging with "another father-in-law" of his. "We will enter Bagh tomorrow," he told us before leaving. "It will be Friday, and the place will be extremely lively."

After Hamesh Gul disappeared, we walked along quietly for a while, until the voice of Tor Baz interrupted my thoughts.

"Friend," he spoke softly, "all this while, I have been wondering what makes a man like you, who has lived in a foreign land, seek out and visit this place and these people? After all, the only memory you have is your father's. This land should have meant nothing to you, as you have not seen or lived in it before."

"It is difficult to explain, Tor Baz," I replied thoughtfully. "It is only a question of feeling, and reasons do not come into it. Let me put it this way: that without knowing my people and my father's land, I have always felt that I did not truly know myself. I think in my place, you would do as I am doing."

"Oh, no, not I!" He snorted derisively, with surprising intensity. "To me only a few things are important, and seeking out one's past is of little consequence. What good comes of looking for it?"

I remained silent. Tor Baz spoke again: "I did not wish to hurt you," he said reflectively. "It is not necessary that I should be right in this matter."

After about one hour's journey, we found Hamesh Gul waiting for us in the middle of the track. He was not alone. With him were two very old men. Both were short and slight in build. Both carried almost identical walnut staffs in their hands, but there the resemblance ended. Old age had defeated the first one. His beard was completely white and rippled like a field of grass with the slightest movement of his head. His right hand, as he shook it with mine, was quivering with palsy, and even his skin had the dull look about it that marks a man moving close to death and being aware of it moment by moment. He was introduced to me by Hamesh Gul as his "second father-in-law."

"You will not meet many of his kind nowadays," Hamesh Gul told me with obvious pride. The old man heard this and accepted the tribute without any change in his expression. The other man was probably as old, but the fear of death was not upon him yet. His beard and mustache indicated regular care and had been dyed with henna. He was one of the ugliest old men I was to see in the area, but his energy and restlessness made him curiously interesting.

"I came down with my friend Mehboob only to

greet you," he said. "It is an honor for us to have eminent guests visit us."

All the while his eyes kept flickering across me, over the animals, to Tor Baz—back and forth. He was madly curious about us. We started off in a single file, the pair of old men leading and Hamesh Gul following behind, after the mules. The path was very narrow, and for most of the distance it lay by the side of a dry ravine. It had suddenly become very dark, as the clouds had gathered overhead and were packing themselves together, seemingly resigned to preparing the daily evening shower for Maidan.

Before we reached Mehboob Khan's house, a very fine drizzle had started. All of us opened our *chaddar*s and wrapped them around ourselves, more as an instinctive gesture than as a conscious protection against being soaked.

The old men slowed down. They hopped over a low wall that I only sensed but did not see in the enveloping darkness. There was a muffled shout, and suddenly a door opened in the night, showing a pale light inside a room. We stepped into it. This was Mehboob Khan's *hujra*—his living room, guest room, conference room, and men's quarters combined into one.

It was a large, sprawling room, bigger than the *hujra*s I had seen so far. There were more than a score of men of various ages sitting around—some squatting on the floor, thickly covered with dried rushes of reeds and grass, others reclining on the string cots scattered against the walls. The two oil lanterns in the room provided very poor light, and only in small pools. Large parts of the room were in shadow, and the feeble efforts of the oil lanterns were blanketed by the smoke streaming from large iron pans full of burning wood.

As we entered, the murmuring died down and the men froze for a moment. I can hardly remember the introductions. I recall only that about a third of the men present were introduced by Mehboob Khan as his sons, most as his nephews, and the rest as guests. I, too, was introduced as a guest and led to a string bed, over which a few pillows and cushions had been laid.

Ghairat Gul, Mehboob Khan's henna-bearded friend, followed me to the same cot. The men went back to doing what they had been doing before we arrived. There was the gurgle of a hookah, the clicking of knitting needles from a man who was making a shapeless sweater for himself, the rustling of rushes in one corner as another made himself more comfortable on the floor, and the room reverted to its old mood.

I took off my sandals and socks, and passed my hands over my sore feet. Some blisters had burst. These patches were raw, and blood had soaked my socks. Hamesh Gul and Mehboob Khan, who had gone inside the house, joined us again. Mehboob Khan shouted an order. Two young men got up from one corner and came toward me. One of them bent down and dragged away a large earthen pan from under my cot and moved it toward another corner. It was full of old, dirty-looking hand grenades. The other picked up one of the braziers by the edges and brought it nearer to my bed.

"Warm your feet over the fire," ordered Mehboob

Khan. "They should be washed and bound tonight." He moved away to another cot, where a place had been made for him. Ghairat Gul remained where he was, warming his hands and feet, cracking his fingers with obvious enjoyment, and continuing his frank examination of me.

As my eyes grew used to the darkness, more and more of the room came into focus, and the people in the shadows started assuming clearer shape and identity. There was the knitter in the corner, clicking away without pause, a group of three men sitting a few paces away from him and passing the hookah around, a group of four sitting around the second fire pan, talking among themselves softly and passing a box of chewing tobacco around. The box had a mirror on the lid, which caught the light from the lamp and flung it back in mad dashes across the room. The rest had rearranged themselves near and around my brazier.

The gloom near the rafters was more difficult to penetrate, and try as I might, I could not make out the two massive objects hanging near the ceiling. Ghairat

Gul caught me looking at them. "You know what they are?" he asked.

"No," I replied after a while.

"They are parts of a plane which Mehboob Khan brought down about fifty years ago. Mehboob Khan and I searched the wreckage for days, but we could not find the special pistol which the pilots carried in those days," he reminisced sadly.

"And every year in those fifty years, I tell you twenty times that I am not sure I brought down the plane." Mehboob Khan's voice was shaking with suppressed anger. "I only know that I fired at it and it dropped after some time. It could have been due to so many other things. We are not young men, Ghairat Gul," he continued, "that we have to boast about things which we may not have done. We should be more than satisfied with what our share of life has been."

"That is so. That is rightly so," agreed Ghairat Gul. The room fell silent. Even the dog, which had been moving restlessly, whimpered to itself and lay down under one of the cots.

The two old men sat staring at the fire, frowning with concentration. I was watching Mehboob Khan. His face in profile did not look like an old man's face. Even his hands had stopped their trembling and lay docilely in his lap. Suddenly, he broke out of his reverie and looked at me with recognition.

"I knew your father," he said. "You should know it. We grew up together. Two youngest sons of two poor families. We drove our flocks together. We started working the fields at the same age. It was together that we made our first bold remarks at some girls and then hid together the rest of the day, worrying whether they would tell their fathers, who would come after us. We shared one gun together, an old matchlock—and we were together when I killed my first man with it. He was an enemy of my father's, and I had crept after him as he was working in the field. When I was near enough, I lit the fuse and aimed the gun. The man saw this and started running. The gun took some time before it fired, and I started running after him, gun aimed at the fleeing figure. Your father found the sight very funny and stood there laughing until the gun finally went off and my father's enemy fell.

"Get me that gun down from the rafters," he told a boy sitting near his feet. The boy scrambled up and brought down an old matchlock with a long, heavy barrel and a thin curved butt. It was dark with age, and the wood below the barrel was splintered. The fuse in the hammer was missing.

"Our paths separated after that. Your father had always been restless. He went away one day without telling anyone and joined the army. I stayed on."

He remained silent for some time. One of the young men moved from the corner and stirred the embers and blew them into small dancing flames. Mehboob Khan looked thoughtfully at the boy.

"Boy," he said, "you are Abdul Malik's son. Are you not?"

"Yes, Uncle," the young man replied.

"It was your grandfather, child, who looked after me when I was your age. He was not a friendly man, and not many people knew him personally throughout

Tirah and even beyond. His reputation was fearful. He was known as one who would be prepared to attempt anything, if only there was sufficient money involved. There were grim tales of how he had acted as a hired assassin in his youth, but in his old age he had steadied and was getting more than enough money from supplying information and doing a few odd jobs for foreign governments.

"He was in touch with Afghanistan, with Turkey, with Belgium and Germany, and even with Russia and China. He was working for all of them, but they did not mind, as he was reliable and dependable in his own way. He must have heard of my circumstances, as he sent for me one day and asked me to do some work for him. It was a simple task, and he paid me when I carried it out. I must have pleased him, because gradually he entrusted more and more work to me, till I was working for him almost the whole time and was being allowed to make decisions on my own. In less than two years, I was a kind of overseer for him and was looking after the work myself.

"Boy, your grandfather died just before the First World War broke out. His spirit must indeed have been unhappy at leaving this world just when his services were needed most. Anyway, as soon as the war started, there was a heavy rush of work. I, too, had to make a choice of who among my various clients had to be treated as the most favored. Gradually, it somehow appeared to resolve itself, and I found myself working almost entirely for Afghanistan, Turkey, and Germany. They considered our area and our people as deserving real importance in those years, and were prepared to spend a lot of money to see that their interests were looked after properly.

"One day—I think it was the time when the war had run half its course—I received a very unusual message from my German contacts. They told me of a scheme which had been dreamed up back in their country to organize our entire tribe to fight against the British. Eight battle standards or flags, one for each of our clans, had been made in Germany, with suitable verses from the Holy Koran embroidered on them. The standards were being sent to us through Turkey and Afghanistan. I was to see that these battle standards were accepted with the honor due to them, and to ensure that each of the clans started using them as symbols against the British.

"Since the idea was something entirely new to our people and I was not clear about how it would work, I sent frantic messages back, asking for more time to sort things out. The reply I received astonished me. I was told that the practicability of the idea should be assumed as sound, because it had originated from a man who lived in Germany and was himself an Afridi. The letter also told me who the Afridi was."

Mehboob Khan looked at me. "It was your father, son. He had deserted from the British to the Germans during the war and was working for them. That was the only time I heard from him after we went our separate ways. I never saw him again, but seeing you has brought joy to me. Though I did not entirely believe in the scheme, I tried to see that it worked. I visited the leading mullahs and explained to them how the clans and the whole tribe needed to be organized if we were to resist the British in a better way than we had been doing in the past. After a lot of talking, we decided on a number of measures. They included electing a king for Tirah who would have his headquarters at Bagh, making people agree to providing the king with some funds. It was agreed that he would receive a pound of opium out of every fifty pounds sold in the area, and that a small select body would be created in every clan who would look after their particular standard, bring it out, and persuade people to rally around it. It took quite a few days to make all the decisions, but we were ready for the flags when they arrived at Bagh.

"The flags entered Tirah before the snow had started falling in the hills. They were accompanied by two foreigners, and the plan almost failed because of this foolhardiness. The British were waiting for this party. Their agents started heavy sniping as soon as the party entered our territory. We had to send the two foreigners back quickly, or the tribes would have risen against us for betraying our homeland to outsiders. As soon as the foreigners left, our people and the men who were siding with the British sat down to talk things out. Do you know who was leading the other side?" he asked me. I was not expected to reply, so I kept silent.

"It was Ghairat Gul, the man sitting next to you. He had me in real trouble then."

Ghairat Gul gave a low laugh and cracked a few toe joints. He was enjoying the warmth of the fire.

"Those were frightening days for me," Mehboob Khan continued reflectively. "I had to argue my case before the assembly of the tribes, while Ghairat Gul's party argued theirs. I knew clearly that if I lost, not only would my reputation suffer, but I would be completely destroyed. I would have to leave my country and live as a lonely outcast wandering in the cities, cut off from my people. I had to keep desperation out of my countenance and to hide my turmoil from the world. I had to sit and laugh and talk, to combine the qualities of an orator—and a witty one at that—with that of a schemer. I had to move at night to win as many friends as I could who would listen to my side of the case the next day. And all this while, I had to slaughter lambs and throw feasts for the assemblage. The *jirgas* went on. One day, there would be a tilt in my favor. Next day, they would lean in favor of Ghairat Gul. My money was almost gone, and I dared not borrow from others.

"My luck seemed to have run out. However, the decision could not be put off much longer, because already the winter migration of our clan had been delayed and the women and children were feeling the bite of the cold.

"The *jirga* gave its decision suddenly one day, in my favor. Two things had swayed the assembly—the standards had verses from the Holy Koran inscribed upon them, and they could not be disgraced; and Ghairat Gul would not, in any case, lose face, because his party had already evicted the two foreigners by force from Tirah."

The old man smiled. He looked at me and said, "It was Ghairat Gul himself who tried to bail me out this way. Do you know why he did it?"

"I cannot even guess," I confessed.

"It is simple. Ghairat Gul did not wish that I be destroyed. His value to the British would have lasted only as long as I existed as a danger to them. Without me, even Ghairat Gul would have been reduced to an ordinary poor Afridi.

"It was a happy outcome for the both of us. The British were pleased with Ghairat Gul. The Germans and Turks with me. The tribes were also pleased, and took to the standards with enthusiasm. They were like children, and wanted to raise them for the simplest things. We had difficulty restraining them and telling them that the gathering of clans must not be treated as a light matter.

"After this, we had the happiest and the most joyful year of our lives. We had money, and we bought land—both Ghairat Gul and I. People talked about us with envy and respect, and children, as they grew, would dream about how they would grow up into another Ghairat Gul or another Mehboob Khan. Of course, all this changed years ago. When men started making fortunes through smuggling or through trading in opium and hashish, boys no longer dreamed about us. They hoped for different things."

He turned to Ghairat Gul. "Do you know," he asked, "our washerman, whose children used to run after scraps, his son is now the richest man in Tirah?"

"I know," replied Ghairat Gul.

"His womenfolk refuse to do the waxwork on the dresses any longer, and they were the only ones who knew how it is done."

Ghairat Gul continued: "Yes, those were good years. The British had won the war. Germany had lost, and Russia was on its knees. Once the British had no worries in their own areas, my work did not end. In fact, I became even busier, and at times had to wander outside the country, undertaking tasks which they set for me."

Ghairat Gul got up and went to a corner, where some dried poppy stalks were lying in a bundle. He broke off a few pods and crushed them between the palms of his hands. They made a crackling sound. He rubbed the mixture between his hands and blew on it to separate the seeds from the shell and started eating them as he walked back to the cot. A couple of other men followed his example, and one of them brought me some seeds, too. I thanked him.

Ghairat Gul sat down and closed his eyes. "The food won't be very long now," said Mehboob Khan. Ghairat Gul opened his eyes and belched—a harsh, guttural belch. He kept staring at the fire and stirred it with the toe of his leather sandal, frowning all the while.

Over food, I asked Hamesh Gul if our program of going into Bagh tomorrow was finalized. "Yes, we will say our Friday prayers there and will also see the flags being raised."

"Why are the flags being raised?" I asked.

"To decide the future of our schools." He realized that I hadn't understood him, and continued: "You see, our elders had approached the government, and on their request the government sanctioned a few schools for our area and engaged teachers to run them.

Some feel that this amounts to a violation of our freedom and independence, and the tribes are to meet tomorrow to decide whether to keep the schools or do away with them."

"Don't you want schools?"

"I do not care one way or the other," he replied. "I am too old to study, anyway, but I shall certainly enjoy being present when both sides argue."

After dinner, Mehboob Khan rose. He looked Hamesh Gul straight in the face and said, "Do you know that if the elders had not asked for schools, the opposite side would certainly have? They are not bitter about the schools, but their anger is against the elders who presumed to speak on their behalf to the government."

He turned to me. "Son," he said softly, "the flags are now with the young people. Tomorrow, they will not be raised against an intruder from outside. They will be raised to humiliate the older men." He wished the others and me a good night and walked slowly out of the room. The others also started leaving in ones and twos until only my companions and I remained to rest for the night. Every time the door opened, I could hear the splash of water pouring down the roof and the hiss of rain as blasts of wind drove it against the mud walls. The moment the door closed, the thick walls muffled all sounds and provided a feeling of security.

I lay awake for a few minutes, reveling in the warmth and the peace that the room offered before drifting off to sleep, and it seemed all too soon when I was woken up for my breakfast the next morning.

I opened the door and went outside for a wash. The rain had stopped sometime during the night, but it was still cloudy. All the nearby hollows and depressions were filled to the brim with water, and even the small crevices in the rocks were stained with moisture. I could not account for the feeling of somberness that overcame me, and hurried back to the warmth I had left behind. Even back in the room, the feeling of emptiness remained, and I could not get rid of it. It seemed to affect my companions also. One or the other would make an effort at conversation, but it would die down quietly.

The mood of the previous evening had gone. I was a stranger, and I felt like one as I said my good-byes. As I left, I wished my last memory of this house had been that of the previous evening, and not of the cold despondency of this morning.

The three of us walked, each absorbed in our own thoughts—perhaps feeling a little lost and bewildered but unable to break the shell enveloping us. It took us three hours to reach Bagh. The sky had lightened a little, but the clouds were still thick enough to stop the sun from shining through.

Tor Baz wanted to visit the shrine of a holy man in the area. "You should come along," he said. "A real unbeliever, a kafir mullah," he added, as a compliment to the holy man. "I met him some years ago. He was a grand old man."

We walked down the only street of Bagh slowly. At one of the first shops we came across, Hamesh Gul insisted on having my bruised foot attended to. The person in charge, whom Hamesh Gul insisted on addressing as "Doctor," opened the previous day's bandages, washed the wounds, and put a layer of hair pomade on them before rewinding the old bandages around the foot. The street was crowded with small groups of men walking unhurriedly, taking their time to curiously look into every shop and at the other people in the street. One of the busiest shops was next door to where I was being ministered to. The owner dealt in opium and hashish, and a number of men were bargaining with him for a good price for the dark, nearly black bricks of the narcotic. Opposite us was a small shop where a middle-aged man was watching his young son eat a tomato, which he had bought for him after prolonged selection from a basket.

Tor Baz stood close to me. Whenever small groups

would pass by, he would whisper in my ear. "That is a neighboring tribe, the Para Chamkanis," he would say. "Have you seen the leggings they are wearing?" Or, "See, those are the Orakzais. I wonder what brings them here. They have their own Bagh."

Then he pointed out a group of bearded men walking past. "There you see some Hindus. They are not allowed by the Afridis to wear white turbans, so they wear colored ones."

He reeled off name after name of the tribes, and of the Afridi clans. There were so many names that they confused me, and after a while I stopped making an effort to remember them. I suddenly began to feel very cold and shivery.

Hamesh Gul, who had been silent for most of the morning, turned to me as my bandaging was completed. "I must go back to Mehboob Khan's house after the Friday prayers. I am to take the mullah with me."

I kept silent. "When are you coming back?" asked Tor Baz.

"Tomorrow, perhaps. After the funeral is over."

"Whose funeral?" I inquired.

"Mehboob Khan's. He died during the night."

"Mehboob Khan is dead?" I repeated incredulously. "Why was I not told?"

"Yes, he is dead. His sons did not wish you to be disturbed. A man that is born must die, and only he who dies without sons dies unhappy. I shall be back tomorrow, if God wills."

"I shall remain with him," Tor Baz told Hamesh Gul.

My shivering was worse now, and my attendants noticed my discomfort with some worry. They insisted we proceed straight to the shrine that Tor Baz had mentioned, and said that my food would be brought there.

The pain became much worse, and I had to walk with the support of my two companions. We passed the main mosque, where a crowd was already collecting for prayers, and we entered the shrine next to it. My companions prayed briefly at the graves and tasted a pinch of salt each before coming back to me.

One of them touched my temples and turned to the other.

"He is burning with fever."

"He will not see the flags raised," said the other.

My shivering did not stop, and I felt ashamed of it. Whenever I opened my eyes, I faced two truck headlights that some devotee had embedded in the cemented grave of the holy man who lay buried here. Sometimes one headlight looked bigger than the other, but I could not keep my eyes open long enough to judge whether one was really bigger than the other.

Out of the darkness that was creeping around me, I heard a crescendo of noise, and I knew that the flags had been raised. I had not been able to see them, but perhaps I would one day. Later, some sounds woke me. I still could not open my eyes, but I could hear a number of people standing and talking around the corner from the room where I was lying. I could not understand most of what was being said, as all the voices seemed to blend into one loud wave of sound. Furious voices were accusing someone of having brought me, a foreigner and an infidel, here and having defiled their land. The crescendo waxed and waned around me. Among the voices, I suddenly heard the voice of Tor Baz.

"Why are you worried about this poor man?" he asked. "Can you not see that he is dying?"

Seven

A Pound
of Opium

On the leeward side of a high boulder, an old gaunt man sat, warming himself over a low peat fire. He had been sitting patiently for the last few hours, protected by the boulder from the icy blasts of wind that portend the advent of winter in Upper Chitral. The wind came rushing in and out of the crevice and around the corners, splattering gravel and small sharp stones against his refuge, making Sher Beg huddle closer to the smoky fire.

Occasionally, he would gather his long white beard in his left hand, bend down, and blow into the smoke until his eyes streamed. Sher Beg was tall, as most of the men of this area were. He would have been handsome even in his old age but for his neck, which was swollen to a grotesque size because of goiter. Fresh raw goatskin strapped to his legs with leather thongs provided a contradiction to the rest of him—an incredible old man with ragged clothes and a hopeless and tired look in his eyes.

Upper Chitral is a land of stone. Wherever you look, the landscape is full of stone. There is a variety of forms, of color and weathering, but there is nothing but stones. In size, they range from small grains of sand to giants as tall as two-storied buildings. Stones in one way or another occupy the thoughts of men in this area, and Sher Beg's thoughts, too, were flitting from one mountaintop to another. There lay the mountain in whose shadow he had been born, lived most of his life, married, begotten children. He would also die there. All around him were the crags where he had grazed his animals, and peaks he had climbed in his early years.

Further distant were the massifs that had provided him with a livelihood in his youth. The backdrop to this panorama was the biggest mountain of them all—the giant Tirich Mir.

The major part of Sher Beg's life had centered on Tirich Mir. He had grown to manhood on its slopes, progressed to head porter after a few expeditions, and was accepted as the key guide year after year. During all these years, Tirich Mir provided him with fodder for his body and for his pride. The climbing seasons were short, but even during the long periods of inactivity, he had dreamed about the giant—planning the routes, the camps, the loads; deciding who to weed out from his teams of porters and who to employ in his stead.

Oh, those were grand years, indeed. When he was not climbing, other men pointed him out to one another and spoke of him as the Tiger. He remembered how his heart had swelled with pride when his wife had insisted on naming their newborn daughter Sherakai—the Tiger's Daughter. A man is lucky if he has one such year. He was truly favored by God for having so many of them.

Year after year, the climbers came. They would vie with one another for Sher Beg's help. He would lead them—young men, middle-aged men, and old ones. He would bring them back, their sometimes torn, bruised, and crippled bodies, and see them off only to welcome them back the next year. After each attempt, it was he who distributed any surplus supplies and clothing among the villagers. Boys and girls, women and men, came to him for the castoffs. They were glorious years. How quickly had they passed.

One year the summit of Tirich Mir was finally conquered. Sher Beg didn't realize what it meant at first. In fact, he celebrated along with the rest of the expedition and was bursting with happiness at the achievement. It was only when he found employment difficult the next year and impossible the year after that he truly understood what had happened. It was not Tirich Mir that had been defeated. It had been his defeat.

A sound interrupted Sher Beg's reverie. A noise that

would have gone unnoticed among the moaning and sighing of the wind if he hadn't been waiting for it for the last few hours. The familiar cackle of the bird. Very slowly, he got up and carefully unstrapped the small crossbow hanging over his shoulders. Taking a small pebble from his mouth, he fitted it into the pouch.

He moved slowly and silently, step-by-step, and peered around the corner. A plump brown bird was sitting on an outcrop a few yards away. The old man lifted his crossbow and took careful aim.

The small pebble hit the rock on which the bird was sitting and shattered itself into small fragments. The brown bird rocketed up in the air and whirred toward the hillside. Its sudden passage frightened a herd of ibex that had been sunning themselves in a mountain cleft. They scampered up the hillside in mincing steps toward higher ground, accompanied by the small tinkling sounds of stones dislodged by their feet.

The hunter returned wearily to the fire and started gathering it in an old tin can that he always carried with him. He was still bent over the fire when the earth started trembling and shaking. Softly, the man cried while he waited for the tremors to subside. He had not tasted meat for two seasons now.

Walking toward the next ridge, Sher Beg turned his thoughts again to Tirich Mir. Yes, he nodded to himself, everything had turned to ashes with the conquest of Tirich Mir. Suddenly, the same villagers who had almost worshipped him ignored him and appeared to look through him when he passed by. Since he could not get his livelihood from mountain climbing any longer, food became more and more difficult to find. His family, who had once walked about with pride, began to feel like hunted animals as the vengeance of the villagers turned against them. A time came when Sher Beg could no longer bear it, and he left his village and family and went away to the plains.

Oh, he remembered now what had happened to Sherakai, the Tiger's Daughter. He had sold her to somebody before he left, for a pound of opium and a hundred rupees.

He spent a number of years in the plains—how many, he could not remember, but it was a long time before he came back. Hard as he tried, he could not live without the mountains. He could not die anywhere else.

On his return, he found his wife faithfully looking after the small patch of land he owned. She was alone. He never dared to ask her about the children in case she was reminded of his failure to provide for them. It was strange, he mused, that he could not remember the names of any of his children other than Sherakai— the one that by rights he should have forgotten.

In Lower Chitral, it had been raining intermittently for the last two days. Gusts of high winds had raged over the mountaintops, breaking the tall pines as they dipped into the defiles. Sometimes they drove the rain clouds toward one valley; now they scattered them, once again bunched them, and drove them to another valley. Winter was coming early this year, and the mountain people were all wondering whether to risk staying for a few weeks longer in their huts in the hope that the pass would remain open or to start moving with their goods, children, and animals on their three-hundred-mile annual journey to the plains. Some of the families, deciding to play it safe, had already started preparations for the move.

In one of the huts three-quarters of the way up a mountain in Chitral, a couple lay in each other's arms. Their youngest child lay at the foot of the string bed. The other two children, both girls, and the mother-in-law occupied the second of the two rooms, which they shared with the chickens during the night. The woman was short and stocky, even by the standards of her tribe. She looked older than her twenty-two years. However, she was full of energy and strength, and the decision to move had caused her no more than the usual worry. It had to be done, and what did it matter if they set off now rather than in a few more weeks?

She never considered herself anything other than

lucky at being where she was. At one time, when she was eight years of age, she had lost all hope. That was when her father had sold her for a pound of opium and a hundred rupees to a local prince.

It had taken her mother another year to save the money to buy her back, and still the prince had refused to let her go. She could even now feel the terror when, at her mother's pleading to spare her child, her owner had laughed coarsely and said, "A child? She is a Sher-akai. I assure you if she can accept a small finger, she will find no difficulty in accepting a man's organ." It had taken prayers, pleadings, and luck—not to speak of her mother's savings—to secure her return, and that, too, not before her master had made an attempt to prove his boast before he lost her. He had failed but mercifully had not damaged her seriously.

Her mother had managed to get her married three years later, and her husband had nursed her carefully for two seasons before taking her to bed, and she had enjoyed his hidden fire. Looking at him, she would never have thought that his bearded, glowering visage could hide so much passion and gentleness. This night, he had woken up again and again, seemingly unsated. She guessed rightly that the thought of not being able to sleep close to each other for the next few months—the duration of their journey—was making him indulge to excess even at the cost of tiring himself for the hard work that had to precede the start of the excursion.

While she lay awake, she planned the loads for each child. The youngest would, of course, have to be carried on her husband's back. Although the girl was five years old, she was too weak to manage the fifteen-mile-a-day stages. Perhaps they should let her walk for a few miles each day, to test her legs and see how soon she would be able to join her sisters in sharing their responsibilities.

She got up together with her husband after a silent agreement to make the most of the early hours of the morning. As she rose, she looked affectionately into the other room, where the older girls were sleeping in sacks, and prayed silently that her mother-in-law's insidious comments on her inability to produce sons would not influence her husband.

These three children were all that had survived out of the five she had given birth to. On the mountain, the survival of the mother and child depended entirely on nature. The timing had to be just right so that the mother did not have to carry the child on the journey during the last days of pregnancy. Most of the children that survived were born immediately on their return to the highlands. If they were born too late, they again found it difficult to survive the downward journey in infancy.

She tried to remember how many of her brothers and sisters had lived. Probably, it was two sisters and three brothers, or was it the other way around? She wondered where they were—dead or alive. Even their names eluded her. Her husband had once talked about a brother of his who, he had heard, was employed in the president's house at Rawalpindi. He had tried to see him once but could not gain admission. That was before their marriage. He had then spent the evening wandering about the town and had picked up the old matchlock gun he liked to carry with him on their travels. She never remembered its having been fired.

So now they would set off in a few days. No pot or pan or rag of cloth could be left behind. Their possessions were neatly divided into head loads and animal loads, their herd of buffalo and cows about twenty strong, the hens perched expertly on the loaded animals, the husband carrying the youngest, and the mother balancing a broken aluminum trunk that was ancient already when her mother gave it to her as part of her dowry.

Walking, walking, and walking, using the roads at night when the law allowed them to, the side trails during the day, the graveyards and small unmarked patches used for hundreds of years by gypsies for resting and cooking. Avoiding the towns and villages where they were not welcome, as the locals said they were dirty, damaged the crops, and were suspicious about their tendency to steal. They carefully skirted the cities, fearing to fall afoul of the police, and spread

out into the plains, where they did menial jobs, working as porters, carriers, scavengers—whatever work
they could find—during the three months before
starting their long trek back to the mountains.

By the time the family crested the ten-thousand-
foot Lowari Top, as the pass was known, they formed
a sizable group. Other men, some without families,
joined them with their cattle as well as sheep and
goats. A group would be less vulnerable to potential
hazards as they debouched onto the plains.

The mischief and harassment began as soon as they
reached the tree line on their descent. Initially, it
caused only minor irritation. They ignored the catcalls
and the epithets shouted at them, and even ignored
the occasional stone flung at them and their animals.
On the third night, however, there was a serious
attempt at stampeding their animals and cutting their
tether ropes. The provocations could no longer be
ignored, and a collective decision was made by the
men to guard the animals at night.

Tragedy struck the group two nights later. There

was a sudden noise of firecrackers, the angry shouts of the men, the screaming of women and children, and the frightened and stampeding animals adding to the pandemonium.

When dawn broke and the men returned after rounding up and counting their animals, they found a few sheep were missing; then they were distracted by the wailing and screaming. They ran toward their tents. When they saw the disarray, they rushed around, frantically trying to persuade the women and children to come out from the undergrowth, where they were cowering. It was then that they discovered that three women were missing—one of them was Sherakai. They searched desperately, but they knew the futility of their actions. Her husband stood in a daze with his three daughters.

There was no way he could look after them. He decided to give his daughters away to be cared for while he searched for his wife. To anyone who agreed to take on the responsibility, he offered two of his buffalo. For the youngest girl, who was presently too weak to walk, he offered three. They were to protect his daughters until the mother was found and could rejoin them.

Tor Baz slept soundly in a wayside inn in a nearby village. He had been given a roving commission and a little money by some gem traders in Peshawar who had learned of a recent discovery of semiprecious stones in the hills, of peridot, tourmaline, and topaz. He was to find out more about the location of these discoveries, about reliable contacts in the area and the correct sale prices. He planned to use the initial money to buy some samples so that the quality of the gemstones could be assessed.

On his way back to Peshawar, after completing his assignment, Tor Baz had decided he would stop at the village of Mian Mandi, a notorious market for slave trading. He had never seen it before. It lay in the area of the Mohmand tribe, but he had an instinct that he might collect some useful information there—traders were always willing to exchange gossip on market days.

He woke from his slumber with the sound of a truck driving down the road. He thought he heard a woman scream but could not be sure. Tor Baz tried but could not fall asleep again, so he got up, put on his shoes, and picked up his bag. He woke up the owner of the inn, drank a cup of tea, and started walking toward the market.

Eight

THE BETROTHAL
of SHAH ZARINA

As one starts off the main road and travels into the valley, there is a steady climb until the track ends about six miles on. At this point, nestling between forest-covered slopes, is a small settlement of houses, some shops, a police post, a school, a dispensary, and a mosque. An unusual sight, as people do not tend to live in villages in these mountains.

In the evening, when the cooking fires are lit, one almost never sees more than two dots of light flickering together at any one spot. What brought this group of buildings and houses together was the unfortunate fact that for years this point was the overnight halt for hunting parties shooting the monal pheasant— a beautiful green iridescent bird that is close to extinction.

The discovery that there were monal pheasants in these parts brought development to the place where Fateh Mohammad, a Gujjar, lived. The yearly visits by local princes and foreign dignitaries encouraged the construction of public buildings made of cement and concrete, with chimneys and glass windowpanes. A small hydropowered generator was also installed.

Among the multitude of tribes inhabiting this frontier region, the Gujjars present a curious enigma. What was curious was that in spite of their large numbers and latent strength, they appeared content to live in the shadow of those around them. To their neighbors, the Gujjars did not seem to exist as a separate tribe or people. Their diffidence and humility had become so ingrained in the course of centuries that they showed no resentment at being treated as an inferior people. Indeed, their stoicism went beyond this.

They submitted to the demands of their more power-
ful and brash neighbors, who denied them the right
to settle their own disputes and extracted taxes and
free labor from them. Harsh restrictions were also
imposed on them as to how they could live and how
they could die.

They lived quiet, tormented lives on windswept
hilltops and dark, narrow mountain defiles, eking out
a living from a soil that was so poor it was unattractive
to all others. Under the custom of the dominating
tribes, the Gujjars could neither own the land they
cultivated nor acquire any other property. All they
possessed were their animals and what little they could
carry.

Centuries of insult had created a trauma in these
people. Very few had any pride left in themselves,
their language, or their culture. The next generation
was being deliberately encouraged by their elders to,
whenever possible, give up their identity and merge
themselves into other ethnic groups. Of their children, few knew their own language—they were happy

if they could learn Pashto with an accent, which would not betray them in Pathan society.

In spite of being such a poor community, even they maintained a careful and complicated hierarchy. Those who possessed buffalo and migrated every year looked down on those who owned only goats. Those with a few patches of land hewn into the high mountainsides would not marry into those who did not have any. There were some who were so poor that they had neither animals nor land nor houses. They lived on charity and were looked on with pity by others.

When the new mosque of stone and cement was being constructed, Fateh Mohammad supervised the work jealously. In fact, he was so critical and demanding that the contractor had several quarrels with him. Fateh Mohammad had, as the local mullah, presumed that the new mosque would be placed under his charge and he would be installed in it. He was to be disappointed, though, because on completion, a short, rubicund man rode up the valley in one of the timber trucks with a letter from the local official, appointing him as the guardian of ecclesiastical affairs. He also brought with him a loudspeaker and had an amplifier set up to sound the call for prayers.

Fateh Mohammad was a very disappointed man. In fact, he soon had a scuffle with the new preacher and got the worse of it. He brooded for some days over what had happened to him, and made plans to blow up the mosque with dynamite. However, after a few days, he resigned himself to his fate and accepted the fact that the new preacher would look after the locals while he would be left with solely that part of his flock that was spread thinly over the mountains.

Only one gesture of defiance remained with him. Every day at dawn, while the amplifier was still warming up, Fateh Mohammad's beautiful voice floated into the air, calling the faithful to prayer. In spite of his best efforts, the new preacher could neither silence Fateh Mohammad nor be the first to announce the call.

Fateh Mohammad lived with his family in one of

the old houses in this small community. The ground floor, a large room usually meant for animals, was occupied by some poor relations of the owner while the first floor was given free of rent to Fateh Mohammad as a gesture of charity and piety. The owner was a young man without a family who had left for the city on being selected as a police constable some years ago.

Fateh Mohammad's children were all daughters. He had eight of them, which included an eighteen-year-old by his first wife, who had died in childbirth. On most days he started early, picking a direction and climbing up, homestead to homestead, calling on his flock. He usually returned late in the evening with his collection, which was always in the form of food, usually maize. For these payments, he had to look after a circumcision rite in one place, a wedding or a funeral at another, perhaps an occasional exorcism. Once in a while, people saw him sitting on his rooftop with his children. On these days, he usually drew a small playing board on the earthen floor and played children's games with them with black and white pebbles.

Since people knew that on these days his family would go hungry, they would bring them food, often stale unleavened bread, which the couple and their ravenously hungry children would consume avidly.

Fateh Mohammad had named his eldest daughter, his firstborn, Shah Zarina. This name was a combination of two words, both denoting aspiration to royal connections. In these mountain areas, the poorer the family, the more high-sounding names it gave its children.

Shah Zarina had been a pretty girl. When she grew up, she might have been described as beautiful. She could usually be seen carrying one or the other of her half sisters straddled on her hip as she walked in and out of the room the family occupied.

There was little that remained secret in this small community. There were no curtains to hide behind, nor screens of any sort. All that a person did, the life he lived, was open to view.

———

The spring thaw was setting in after the winter of usual desperation and misery. After each family had withdrawn themselves, the community was beginning to bestir itself. There was a noticeable air of hope that for the next few months, life would be easier. There would be work to do, and the constant torment of hunger would fade to a certain degree.

One night Fateh Mohammad's wife went out to wash herself. When she returned, she roughly shook her husband awake. "Come out!" she said, shaking with excitement. "Spring has started." Fateh Mohammad rolled the thin quilt around himself and followed his wife out of the room.

There was a full moon, and it hung half hidden behind the northern cliff. The moonlight was strong and dazzling to the eyes. His wife silently pointed at the moon. A long distance away on the mountain crest, he could see small antlike figures silhouetted against its orb.

There was a long chain of them moving slowly with loads on their backs. These were the ice cutters. They were men who lived in the highest village, whose main occupation was cutting blocks of ice from the glaciers and carrying them on their backs down into the valley, where waiting trucks loaded them up and sped away to the cities, to people living in the warmer regions.

The children, who had pretended to be asleep during their parents' lovemaking, had also trooped out and laughed and clapped their hands at the thought of spring, which would soon be there. They knew that along with the ice cutters, there would also be temporary villages set up of mushroom collectors—men who moved for a few weeks with the snow line, picking up the profusion of mushrooms, drying them, and selling them for export to foreign countries.

Behind all this pent-up excitement lay the fact that every year, at this time, Fateh Mohammad undertook a visit to these relatively affluent groups, who made their payments in cash and cast-off clothes.

The family did not sleep that night. They spent the next few hours talking about and making preparations for Fateh Mohammad's journey. They laughed as they took out his traveling shoes and mended them, joking among themselves as they packed his traveling bag with a few clothes and some books, and also the charms and amulets that these rough-bearded ice cutters favored. Fateh Mohammad started early with his staff in his hand, and at dawn, when he turned to say his prayers, he found that his house was no longer in sight. He felt sad because he was sure that his family must have been waiting to catch sight of him before the next stage of his ascent.

He climbed steadily the whole day, and all the while he kept thinking of his family and about himself. As he heard the movement of buffalo chewing their cud on the ground floors of the houses next to his path, he asked himself why he didn't have any. While passing the huts with water mills, he remembered his own childhood, when he had inquired of his father, also a mullah, why they could not live in a hut with water running through it. His father just looked at him but did not reply. As a child, he had gradually realized that whatever his father may have pretended to believe, their family was living on charity. With the clear-mindedness of the young, he had also grasped that other people's charity to them, though not forced, was grudgingly won by his father with a mixture of chicanery and fear. One day, he frightened his congregation with his imagery of divine wrath. Another day, he would assuage the misery of their lives with glorious visions of ultimate heavenly bliss, where houris gamboled about.

In the innocence of youth, he had imagined that he would not be a hypocritical mullah like his father, but would break away. But before he was too old, he realized with some little fear that his life would be no different from his father's. He learned the scriptures and prepared himself for the life of a mullah, wondering whether his father, too, in his childhood had thought of breaking away but had given up his struggle when he found the mesh too strong.

Fateh Mohammad climbed steadily. He climbed through strands of pines, crossed clumps of wild olives and holy oak protecting the graveyards. On reaching the fir line, he rested for his prayers, ate some dried bread, and washed it down with sweet springwater, and was ready to start up again. The night he spent on the rush-covered floor of a mosque, and was up early next morning for the final stage of his trip.

With the man of the house away on a promising journey, the rest of his family—even the young girls— went about with their heads held a little higher than they had during the winter. They were all aware that on Fateh Mohammad's return they would not have to, at least for a short period, worry about hunger as they did during the winter. With the fear of hunger temporarily banished, none of them felt as hungry as they did when the prospects were grimmer. Fateh Mohammad's wife and daughters chattered and laughed while they worked during his absence. They spent the days cleaning the one room they had. They mixed buffalo dung and mud, and plastered the floor and walls. They ground some borrowed ocher and brick dust, and drew flowers and ancient patterns of birds, which had been handed down from mother to daughter.

They repaired their clothes, cutting patches from torn and discarded garments and sewing them onto the outfits they were wearing. All of them were aware that when the man of the house returned from his trip, he would be a happy man, and it would be a joyous and happy house for some time. Even his morning call for prayers would have a lilt in it, and would not end with a lingering note of sadness as it echoed between the hills.

Fateh Mohammad returned one afternoon. His family spotted him when he was some distance away. They all wanted to step out and watch him walk toward them. He, too, wished to hurry home after his long absence. Yet neither could show their eagerness, as it might cause ribald comments or even a reputation of imprudence. So both sides pretended a casualness toward each other, and it was only in the late evening, when they were by themselves, that they could express their joy at their reunion.

Fateh Mohammad was more cheerful than normal. After remaining mysterious for a while, he broke the news. In one of the communities of ice cutters, he had met a young man who had captured a bear during the winter and had trained it to perform.

This young man had asked for the hand of Shah Zarina. The negotiation about the bride price had been successful, and the marriage would be taking place after one month. There was tremendous excitement in the family. To find a match for the eldest girl with a man of independent means was something they had dreamed and hoped for, but they could have never expected such a miracle to come about during a visit to the ice cutters.

Fateh Mohammad had brought a part of the bride price in advance with him. With this in hand, the family started their preparations. The selection and stitching of the bridal dress, which would last the girl for the better part of her married life, some utensils, and even a little tinsel to sew on for the festive occasion. They also bought provisions for the coming marriage feast.

Exactly a month later, the bridegroom's family came down to Miandam. The groom was a dour young man who was spotted by the guests straightaway, as he was leading a shambling bear with a nose ring, which he tied to a tree, patting it on the head before coming to the house. His father and brothers were carrying ice blocks and insisted on taking them to the trucks before joining the company.

"We did not wish to waste the trip," they explained.

The father counted out the balance of the bride money and handed it over to Fateh Mohammad before the wedding ceremony started. As soon as they had eaten their food, the father wished his son good luck with the bear, and together with his other sons started back for their village. On the way, they remembered that they had not even seen the bride, and hoped that their brother would return one day and look them up and—if he did—would also bring his wife.

In Fateh Mohammad's house, Shah Zarina's cheeks were burning with the bantering she was being subjected to, particularly from the married women. They were teasing her about the ways of a husband. At the same time, they were openly envious of her good fortune in escaping to the city. The husband remained in the village for another day, and spent the night under the tree next to the bear.

The next morning, he walked up with the bear to Shah Zarina's house, where she waited for him with her few utensils and other possessions tied in bundles. As they saw him coming, her sisters and stepmother broke out crying, as is usual on such occasions. Gathering her bundles, she placed them on her head, stepped out of the house, and started walking behind her husband. A few children and women accompanied her some distance but turned back when the bridal pair reached the bridge, beyond which the road began.

The party—the husband and the bear in front, and Shah Zarina with her dowry on her head bringing up the rear—walked mile after mile. Every time they approached a village, she would drop farther behind, as noisy children would collect around the bear and walk along with it until the village was left behind. Once in a while someone would bargain with her husband and a performance would begin. The bear would shuffle around in a dance, imitating an old man, growling, and having a mock fight with his master, alongside various other tricks of entertainment— some mocking, some tragic, and some serious—for the fee that had been agreed on. Her husband accompanied the performance in a singsong while explaining to the spectators what the bear was doing.

Shah Zarina was frightened when passing through the villages. It was not only the boisterousness of the village lads. Once or twice, the village dogs came together and tried to attack the bear while the villagers looked on, laughing. The first time this happened, she felt cold and lonely, because her husband was desperately trying to defend the bear and she had to protect herself and her dowry. As she stumbled about among yelping dogs and jostling strangers, there were a few stray remarks directed at her, which her husband chose to ignore.

At one place—a big village—some schoolboys who had been entertaining themselves by throwing eggshells and mud at an old madman, who was scurrying about in small circles and giggling, diverted their attention to the bear and its owner. Her man bore the first assault patiently while some eggshells and mud landed on them, but then the boys became more vicious. They began throwing stones, and one of them hit the bear on his snout and drew blood. The bear screamed with pain, and at that, her husband took his staff and hit at the boys and managed to disperse them.

They walked on. Her husband bought some flour

from his day's earnings, and they stopped in the afternoon for a rest. She opened her bundles and prepared the evening meal for the three of them. In the towns, the pattern of life changed completely. Here the husband would rent a room on the outskirts, which would be used by the bear at night and Shah Zarina during the day, when the husband was away.

In the mornings after the bear left, Shah Zarina would clean the room and bring in her few belongings and spread them out. In the afternoons, they had to be put together, tied up, and removed so as to have the room ready before the bear returned.

She would then prepare the meal, cooking large quantities of bread, which would last for the bear's morning meal the following day. In town after town, life followed the same pattern. She could not understand why the bear had to have a room and they could not. Once she asked her husband. He looked at her coldly and said, "I can get another wife but not another bear." She was bewildered.

As the months passed, Shah Zarina's dislike for the

bear grew into a dark and sullen hatred. She did realize that she should also consider the bear to be important, but a part of her became jealous at the thought of being considered second to the animal. At the beginning, her rebellion took the form of small gestures that were known only to her. One day she would pour water in the corner where the bear was tied and imagined it passing an uncomfortable night. Another day, she scattered some thorns on the floor. Over a period of time, even this kind of pernicious mischief paled, and she resorted to more vicious tactics. She mixed red chilies with the flour when she baked the bread for the bear. That night, the bear went hungry.

Finally, she hammered small nails at the end of the staff her husband used to beat the bear with every morning to ensure good behavior during the day. That morning the bear got a few sharp cuts instead of the usual harmless blows. When the bear screamed in pain, her husband became worried, and on inspecting the staff, he noticed the small nails. He looked at Shah Zarina, who could not hide her smile. At that, her husband took the same staff and gave his wife exactly the same number of blows as he had given the bear.

From then on, Shah Zarina's life underwent another change for the worse. Her husband made sure that Shah Zarina would not get another chance to hurt the animal. This he did in a coldly logical way, by insisting that she would live a life no more comfortable than that of the bear. If the bear ate his food, so did Shah Zarina. If it chose to go hungry, so would she. If the bear stayed awake during the night, Shah Zarina could not join her husband in the only quilt they had. In the morning, along with the bear, Shah Zarina would get her day's beating.

After a few months of this, Shah Zarina broke down and ran away from her husband. Four days later, she was back in her village, having walked most of the way. She had left her marriage gifts behind, and her suit of clothes with the tinsel still on them was dirty and soiled.

When Shah Zarina returned, she did not hide her

fate, and the whole community mourned with her. The women visited her and cried, while she screamed and pulled her hair. The men met Fateh Mohammad and commiserated with his misfortune. They clucked their tongues sadly. Though having seen only one bear trainer in their lives, they spoke about the infamy of this class in general, and agreed among themselves, wasn't it foolish for a father to marry his daughter to one?

Commiseration for Shah Zarina and her family did not last long. Tongues started wagging. "We only know her side of the story. What if she has not run away but has been thrown out by her husband?"

"What if her reasons for running away are not what she said?"

"Her sisters' marriages will pose problems because of her wayward habits."

Shah Zarina suffered in silence. One night, as she lay awake, she heard her parents talking in loud whispers. She stayed still and overheard snatches of their conversation. "She sits brooding all day, eating more than any of her sisters do. She hardly does any house-work," her stepmother complained.

"Her husband is bound to come by any day. He will demand that she be handed over to him. That is his right. If we refuse, he will ask for the return of the bride price," added her father.

"But we have already spent the money!" her step-mother whined.

"She has created a terrible problem for us all."

Shah Zarina was crushed by what she heard. She picked up the rough woolen blanket and her shoes, and walked silently out of the house and into the night.

When the sun broke in the morning, Shah Zarina was walking aimlessly on a road running beside the left bank of the Swat River. A shout stopped her in her tracks—only a few yards ahead, she saw a man and a woman resting on a sack. The man stood up and came toward her.

"What are you doing, girl, walking by yourself at this time? There should be a brother, or a husband or father, walking beside you. A girl needs protection."

The sight of another woman, though her eyes were inscrutable, provided some strength.

"I have run away from my family. I have no one to walk beside me. I do not know what to do and where to go," she said guilelessly.

"My name is Afzal Khan," said the man. "I may be able to help you, as I am helping this distant cousin of mine. We are going to a place where rich and generous people come to employ help for their houses—like cooks and kitchen maids. They pay well and are kind to those they employ."

Shah Zarina nodded wearily. "I need employment. I can work hard." Afzal Khan placed his hand on Shah Zarina's shoulder.

"Good. Now that is settled. We shall stop at the first place where we can have some tea and get something to eat. You will tell me your story, as I shall have to tell it to the person who employs you."

Nine

SALE COMPLETED

Afzal Khan, who was small and handsome, had been walking with the two women for nearly five hours. The last hour had been particularly uncomfortable, with the sun glaring down on the treeless countryside and not the faintest breath of breeze. With each step, a small puff of dust rose from the ground and seemed to hang, suspended in the air. For as far as the eye could see, the trail of dust created by their feet pointed to where their journey had started.

Afzal Khan was feeling the strain. The heat, the dust, and the fatigue were telling on him, and he had been perspiring profusely, particularly under the dome-like skullcap that men of the Mohmand tribe usually wore. This made him all the more aware of the plight of his companions, who were wearing dirty white cotton burkas, the heavy shroudlike garments that served to hide a woman's body and veil her face. The women, who had been chattering among themselves in the morning hours, had fallen silent.

Afzal Khan turned to them. "We shall stop soon for midday," he told them. "We all need a rest. There is a good kebab shop beyond the next rise." The women nodded in agreement, too tired to respond more enthusiastically. In muffled voices, they told him to stop so that they could urinate before they reached the village. Afzal Khan stopped, and the women went behind a rock. Likewise, Afzal Khan unslung his rifle, untied his baggy trousers, and, facing the other way, urinated while squatting. He then took a few pebbles and dried the last drops of urine before retying his voluminous trousers.

As he waited for the women to reappear, Afzal

Khan thought affectionately about the two of them. They had borne the strain admirably, and without a word of complaint. Shah Zarina had really surprised him. She was young and frail-looking, and for her to bear the journey so well proved beyond any doubt that her stock was sound and that she had the grit, the inner strength, and the endurance that make a woman pleasing. He was half tempted to keep her but frowned at such foolish thoughts. If he started behaving so irresponsibly, he could end up a pauper without too much effort. After all, there were Mohmands better looking than he who had been fated to spend their lives chopping firewood day after day in big cities such as Peshawar and Karachi.

The women joined him after a while, and the party started on its way again. This was their third day on the road. From the verdant and heavily wooded land of Swat, they had climbed down onto the plateau of Malakand, with its irrigated orchards and fields. From then on, it had been a steady progress toward desolation. Fields, cultivation, vegetation had faded miles ago, and the land was now bleak, hot, and dusty. It looked like the middle of nowhere—small, dry hills with tufts of coarse grass sprouting here and there, narrow ravines intersecting the landscape, marking the angry passage of flash floods every year when the rains fell. Afzal Khan knew the country well. "Put him anywhere," his friends would claim, "blindfold him, and he will still guide you by the smell in the air, by feeling the soil with his feet."

As Afzal Khan had predicted, the moment they crossed the next rise, the village of Mian Mandi, nestling in the hollow of the hills, suddenly came into view. It was not very impressive to look at—a collection of huts, smaller than those in more prosperous villages, huddled against one another. There was a pool of water on one side of the village, which was reflecting the sun like a mirror, and dark black smoke rose thickly from a hut next to it.

"That must be the kebab shop," remarked Sherakai, the older woman, to no one in particular. It did not take the party very long to walk down to the village.

Afzal Khan took his women straight to the shop, where he made them sit down on a wooden bench lying under an awning made out of reeds and grass.

The owner of the shop sat cross-legged next to a large frying pan, engrossed in scraping burned bits of mincemeat from its edges while the oil sizzled. Small tendrils of smoke rose from the pan and added to the aroma of burned animal fat. He looked up as Afzal Khan walked up to him.

"Two *seer* of kebab and some hot bread," ordered Afzal Khan. "Make them ready while I go and say my afternoon prayers. Also, send some water for the women. They might wish to wash the dust off."

After giving these instructions, Afzal Khan walked away toward the pond, which was the major source of water for this area. He sat down near the edge, removed some pieces of scum floating on the surface with a stick, and started washing his arms, face, and feet meticulously.

As soon as he had finished his prayers and returned to the shop, platters of food and a jug of water were set before them by a young boy whose looks and gait suggested that he was serving his owner's physical needs as well. He made eyes at Afzal Khan and fluttered his long eyelashes at him.

"How long are you staying?" he asked softly.

"What day is it?" countered Afzal Khan.

"It is Monday, today."

"Then I shall have to stay for three days."

They smiled secretly at each other. Thursday was the sale of women.

"Where can I get a room for us?" Afzal Khan asked.

"We have some rooms, my master and I. I shall talk to him. He listens to me."

When the boy left, the women slipped their veils off their faces and started to eat from a common plate. Sherakai's face was puckered with distaste. "He is a catamite." Her peasant morality was shocked at such a blatant exhibition of perversion. Afzal Khan looked reflectively at the sturdy-looking woman sitting opposite him. Her lower jaw was a little too heavy, and the

faint smudge of dark hair on her upper lip was promi-
nent because of her fair skin.

"You find all kinds of people in this world," he told
her. "May God forgive all sinners." After the food was
finished, he got up and threw the scraps on the floor.
A mangy bitch that had been feeding her pups in one
corner rushed out and started groveling for food on
the mud floor.

Lifting his shirt, Afzal Khan took out a plastic wal-
let from the waistcoat he wore underneath.

"What do I owe you?" he asked the tavern keeper.
"Have you arranged for a room?"

"Two beds should be enough. The women should
be able to sleep together. If they want to sleep separately, I shall get another bed later on," he answered.

"The boy will show you the way. By the way, I do
not rent him out," he whispered to Afzal Khan, handing him the change. The young boy led the party to
where their rooms were. As they turned the first corner, Afzal Khan looked back. The kebab shop's owner

sat hunched over his pan, intent on scraping the burned bits of meat from it and preparing for the next customer.

The boy unlatched one of the rooms in a mud-walled courtyard and took two string cots from the storeroom and threw them inside. "I hope you like the room," he chirruped.

"We do," acknowledged Afzal Khan. "Get us some bedding."

"I can offer you my own," responded the boy coquettishly. Laughing to himself, he went away and returned after a short while with some cotton sheets and pillows. "The drinking water is in the room next door, and if you need anything else, just call me." He was addressing Afzal Khan but talking to the women. There was pity in his voice as he offered them his help. Another two faces to add to the multitude in his memory, growing with the passage of each Thursday. Women, some little more than infants, some already on the threshold between middle and old age; some who laughed at their fate and others who never stopped crying. Some who appeared once and then vanished completely. Others came again and again, sold sometimes to one man and then to another. There were those who had run away from their husbands or their fathers and those who were running away from life. His memory was only a sea of women's faces, and his small body shook with tension every time he saw yet another face destined to be sold. Yet it was strange that the women had always shown loathing and hatred toward him. He could feel it now, in the two women standing before him.

As the next two days passed, the rooms in the courtyard quickly filled up: sometimes a lone man with just one woman shambling behind him, and sometimes two or three came together who had joined up on the trails leading to the hamlet. The women were always carrying some possessions from their past lives in small, pitiable bundles. One walked with glazed eyes, carrying a blue flower vase in her hands like a candlestick. Another strode along proudly, carrying her man's rifle on her shoulders. There also came men who brought no women. They came to buy and had nothing to sell themselves.

Before the second day was over, the inn was surrounded by small tents, set up and hired out to the visitors. While the men used up the time wandering about, looking at the wares of others, laughing and jesting with old acquaintances, Afzal Khan's women remained in their room except when they went out together to the hillside, when the stars were still glimmering. The monotony of their days was only broken by meals of tea and kebabs brought for them twice a day by Afzal Khan.

With the influx of people, the kebab shop did roaring business. The owner had brought out his transistor and played it the entire day without interruption, not even switching it off for the news or the cricket match commentaries in English. His shop provided a comfortable meeting place for men who had gathered from all corners of the country—groups of them lounging about, chewing and spitting tobacco, some sitting on wooden benches and chairs, others on string cots that had been dragged out and placed in the open. The eating of kebabs and drinking of tea seemed to go on without interruption. The tavern's mongrel bitch and her pups, no longer hungry, looked disdainfully at the scraps lying on the ground.

Afzal Khan was approached by several men, at one time or another, who made inquiries about his women. Some he brushed away brusquely, as he instinctively recognized them as scavengers—found wandering from one village to another, from one market town to the next, trying to manage on the scraps thrown to them either as charity or as commission for acting as go-betweens. There were others with whom he was more patient, though he knew they were small men who could not afford the price he had placed on his women. There were only three men whom he recognized as good customers. He knew two of them of old, as they were regular suppliers to the city brothels, and the third was a young man whom he had not seen before. He appeared to be interested in Shah Zarina, and had not been frightened away at her price, though he did express considerable indignation.

Afzal Khan explained the circumstances of both the women to the customers. Sherakai, he told them, had been kidnapped in a raid but had escaped and returned to find that her husband had taken a younger wife, who had borne him a son. Her mother-in-law, who had never approved of her, lost no opportunity in harping on her failure to provide sons to the family.

As the weeks passed after her return, Sherakai grew more and more frantic. Her mother-in-law's glee knew no bounds. If the new wife had merely felt happy and had forgotten Sherakai in her victory, it would have been all right. But where there had been only taunts and innuendos to contend with earlier, the new wife and her mother-in-law tried to devise all kinds of ways to hurt her cruelly and make her a figure of ridicule and contempt. Then one day they beat her with sticks in front of her daughters, and laughed when she cried out.

"After that, she ran away, and I happened to come

her way," said Afzal Khan. "She claims that she fell in love with me and wished me to carry her off, but I think she prefers humiliation from total strangers than by those she knows. You may rest assured that she will make a cheerful and willing worker," he told the brothel agents. "She will forget her daughters in no time."

He was more reticent about Shah Zarina, and admitted that he himself did not know anything about her beyond what she had told him herself. And all she had mentioned was that she had no one to protect her, and that all the village lads were treating her as fair game. Things had come to such a pass that she could not venture alone in the fields without someone or the other trying to tease or assault her. If she complained, the whole village charged her with loose morals—if she didn't, the men became bolder. So one day she had just run away, got a lift from a passing truck driver, and disappeared.

"I believe she is a virgin so far," said Afzal Khan. "And if I could help it, I would rather sell her for marriage."

"So she is not in love with you, Afzal Khan?" one of the traders said, and laughed.

"Not so far," he countered. "But if I try, she would not resist me."

On the third day, the discussion took a more serious turn. The price of Sherakai was agreed on without too much difficulty. Both the traders agreed to merge their interest and purchased her jointly in equal share. The negotiations for Shah Zarina were more exacting. As a virgin, she was a pearl, and any man would have liked her on his string bed, but the traders appeared reluctant to pay the price Afzal Khan was demanding, and he was not willing to reduce it.

During one of the intervals between negotiations, the unknown young man, whom Afzal Khan had taken a liking to the previous day, came to him again and started talking about Shah Zarina and the difficulties of completing the sale.

"Did I hear you say that you would prefer to sell her for marriage?" he asked.

"That I would," replied Afzal Khan. "She is a right one for marriage. She would be willing to die for the sake of her man and her home."

"I think so, too," said the young man softly. "But I am not rich enough to pay the sum you are asking."

"How much do you offer?"

"All I have on me is three thousand rupees. I only wish I had more."

Afzal Khan thought for a while and then spoke out: "I will accept your three thousand rupees. Treat the rest as my marriage gift. It goes against my grain to enter into such a foolish bargain, but let not men say that Afzal Khan was unwilling to lose money when it was required of him."

The young man's face broke into a wondrous smile. He took Afzal Khan's hands and kissed them, counted out the three thousand rupees, and put them in Afzal Khan's pocket.

"Take me to her."

Afzal Khan walked with the young man to the

small room where Shah Zarina was sitting by herself after the departure of her companion. He called her to come out and made her face the young man.

"I have sold you for marriage. This young man is going to marry you. May God keep you happy."

She was standing before a man dressed all in black. The end of his turban had been looped under his chin and tucked back into the headband. He was short—hardly as tall as Shah Zarina herself.

His jet-black beard and a few stray locks struggled free from the confines of his turban. Shah Zarina turned her glance back to Afzal Khan.

"I thank you," she said simply. "I shall always pray for you."

The next morning, the buyers and the sellers started leaving as they had come. Singly and in small groups, they scattered, leaving the village behind as they had found it—a sleepy collection of huts with no sounds, no music, and hungry dogs roaming about—until it would start coming to life with the approach of next Thursday.

On one of the trails, Tor Baz walked along with Shah Zarina behind him, and fingered the small silver amulet that was stitched to the inside of his cloak. He was smiling, as he did most of the time. While he usually smiled about nothing in particular, this time he was smiling about Afzal Khan.

It's almost incredible, he thought, *that Afzal Khan really believed I would marry this girl, to think of such an old veteran falling for the oldest trick in the trade. The man must really be growing old. Incredible—incredible, indeed.*

But then, he thought, as he walked and remembered the bearded mullah from his childhood nightmares, who had talked about the veils between man and God, *I could settle down with this one. Who but God knows what the future holds for me and for this land? Maybe it is time now to end my wanderings.*

Acknowledgments

The publication of this book would not have been possible but for the persistent encouragement of my brother Javed Masud, the relentless efforts of Faiza S. Khan of the Life's Too Short Short Story Prize, and the deep interest manifested by Meru Gokhale of the Penguin Group. I also want to thank Imran Kureshi for his initial editing of the manuscript.

Jamil Ahmad was born in 1931 and educated in India and Pakistan. He joined the Civil Service of Pakistan in 1954 and served mainly in the Federally Administered Tribal Areas. He was also development commissioner for the Frontier and chairman of the Tribal Development Corporation. Ahmad was posted as a minister in Pakistan's embassy in Kabul at a critical time before and during the Soviet invasion of Afghanistan. After his retirement from the Civil Service, he was a consultant on Afghanistan for four years with the World Bank. He lives in Islamabad with his wife, Helga Ahmad, a nationally recognized environmentalist and social worker.